Deadly Search
A Sheriff Lexie Wolfe Novel

Donna Welch Jones

Book 2, 2nd Edition

TWISTED PLOT PUBLISHING

Deadly Search is a work of fiction. Names, characters, places, and incidents are products of the author's imagination or are used fictitiously and are not to be construed as real. Any resemblance to actual events, locales, organizations, or persons, living or dead, is entirely coincidental.

Twisted Plot Publishing
21938 So. Hickory Lane
Tahlequah, Okla. 74464

© 2017, Donna Welch Jones

All Rights Reserved. No part of this publication may be reproduced, stored in a retrieval system, or transmitted in any form or by any means, electronic, mechanical, recording or otherwise, without written permission, except in the case of brief quotations embodied in critical articles and reviews.

Manufactured in the United States of America

ISBN: 978-0-9970148-7-7
Also available in Kindle eBook

Visit the author's website:
www.donnawelchjones.com

Dedication

To My Parents
Wayne and Wilma Welch

And My Siblings
Sheril Chapman
Lawrence E. Welch
Jeffrey W. Welch

Prologue

Fifteen Years Ago

"You damn fool! My daughter's face is ruined, thanks to your blundering."

His response was an agitated whimper on the other end of the phone line. "You said she wouldn't be home."

"It doesn't matter what you think I said. Lexie's a stubborn little bitch. She refused to go shopping with me. A real man would've been ready for anything, even a teenager jumping on his back."

His voice softened, "Margo, you said you loved me but as long as Nodin was alive you'd remain with him. I killed him for us."

"I'll go nowhere with an idiot. Now I'm saddled with a fortune in doctor bills and an ugly teenager." Margo slammed the phone onto its cradle.

Thanks to the medication, Lexie didn't stir. Her long black hair was shaved on the right side past the temple where the knife cut extended from her cheek. A swollen mask of bruises and stitches distorted the face of her once beautiful daughter.

Margo entered the hospital restroom and peered at her own face. Her daughter's fate left her fearful that she, too, could lose her beauty. The mirror revealed the same lovely blue eyes as her daughter. Margo's face was as perfect as ever. A touch of red was added to her lips. The handsome doctor would soon check on Lexie. Now that Margo was a widow, every man was fair game.

Chapter One

The library basement turned into a pit of swirling dust particles as Lexie pulled out another box of old Diffee newspapers. She sneezed with such force that her waist length braid toppled from the loose bun on the top of her head.

With no success, she'd gone through stacks for the three-month period before her father, Nodin, was murdered. Now she was checking the month after and beyond.

Even a small lead would offer a glimmer of hope. What was the advantage of being the Diffee Sheriff if she couldn't avenge her father's death? Nodin's murderer had roamed free for the last fifteen years. The man who had stabbed her father and left a jagged knife wound down the side of her face at sixteen, was probably confident that he had gotten away with murder.

She pulled the next box of newspapers to a rug that was a mass of frayed yarn and worn spots. Her butt appreciated a reprieve from the hard wood chair she had perched on during the previous four hours.

A bookshelf packed with old Collier Encyclopedias served as her backrest while she continued her search.

The basement was where all things paper came to die in Diffee, Oklahoma. It was a dungeon of forgotten words, volumes that were replaced by Google search. The small country town accumulated much history, all of which was stacked in floor piles and on shelves that extended to the ceiling.

The first week of newspapers after Nodin's death yielded nothing. Her blue eyes watered from the dust and strain of small letters in a darkened room.

There on the obituary page, two weeks after the murder, a short article caught her eye. A man named Chadwick Hawk was killed on Cherokee land by an unknown assailant. Hawk and her dad were approximately the same age at the time. Like her father, he was full-blooded Cherokee and a competitive Indian dancer. An arrow through the heart killed Hawk. It was a very different choice of weapon from the knife that killed Nodin, but it was still worth investigating.

Her hope came out as a sigh. The next edition and the one after revealed nothing. Another two weeks of news passed before the paper followed up on Hawk's murder. Lexie scanned the words.

'The Cherokee Nation Marshal Service reported no leads in the murder of Chadwick Hawk. Inadequate evidence resulted in the release of the only suspect, Leroy Grass. The suspect was known to harass Hawk in apparent attempts to force the victim out of Indian dancing competitions.'

"I got my lead," Lexie said aloud. A frightened gray mouse sprang from a curled corner of the rug.

Lexie observed the tiny critter. "Well, I really wasn't talking to you, but since you showed up, I'll inform you that I don't plan to disturb you anymore today or ever, with any luck."

Heavy feet tromped down the steps and drowned out her mouse conversation.

"Who you talking to, Lexie? Gone psycho sister on me?"

"Talking to a mouse."

"Okay," Tye's dark eyes squinted as he shook his head.

"I finally have a lead."

Tye grasped her hand and pulled her up. "Don't tell me the mouse is an informant."

"Very funny. A man named Chadwick Hawk was murdered about the same time as Dad. Maybe the same man murdered both of them."

"How did the mouse respond to the good news?"

"Ran off."

"What next?" Tye asked.

"I'll talk to Larry Prather at Cherokee Nation. Eventually, I'll question Leroy Grass. Do you want to come along?"

"No deputy duties for me today. I'm driving to Missouri to hunt down the attorney who handled Adam's adoption. Before that, I'll explain to Adam why Jamie and I gave him up for adoption. Tough day ahead."

"I hope it goes well," Lexie offered.

"Me, too. Don't get yourself in a mess before I get home."

"Not me."

Chapter Two

Tye drove his black Chevy Avalanche toward Jamie's house. His mind stewed over his mess. Since Adam found out Tye and Jamie were his biological parents, he avoided them. Three months of cold shoulders were enough. It was time to confront Adam and make him understand why he was given up for adoption.

Adam hesitantly agreed to meet with his parents, probably because Tye told him he wanted his help in the search for Adam's twin. Tye understood the boy's commitment to Dr. Carr who took Adam in after his adoptive parents died in a plane crash, but surely the twenty-year-old could find some place in his life for biological parents.

When Tye pulled into Jamie's driveway, he was relieved to see that Adam showed up. The boy waited in his old red truck.

"Glad you came, Adam."

The young man's eyes examined the ground. "Curious," was his only comment.

Jamie greeted the pair at the door. She wore black jeans and a T-shirt decorated with the black and yellow logo of the Stingers, the college basketball team she coached.

Adam flopped his long, thin body into an old recliner.

His parents sat on a beige and blue striped sofa across from him. The room was so quiet that Tye thought the others could hear his heart beating.

Jamie, his tough girlfriend, didn't seem the least bit strong today. Adam had her hair color—a light fudge shade. His nose was small like hers, but he had Tye's earthen skin color, sculptured cheekbones, and dark eyes. It wasn't difficult to see the Cherokee in his son.

Jamie's voice slowly combined words that she had obviously rehearsed. "Adam, I ask for your forgiveness. I was seventeen and single when I got pregnant with twins. I didn't know that, twenty years later, my greatest regret would be that I didn't fight my father to keep you and your brother."

Adam's head lowered. Tye's eyes couldn't read his expression to assess his response to Jamie's words.

She continued, "You boys are the most important things that have come from my life. My heart was broken twenty years ago. You and your brother are the only two who can help me heal." Tears etched paths down her cheeks.

Adam stood, his smug expression dissolved. "Don't cry, Mom. I understand, and I forgive you."

A sob burst from Jamie's throat. A mixture of disbelief and joy flooded her face. Adam called her mom, something she'd never allowed herself to dream of hearing.

Tye stood beside his son and pulled Jamie to her feet. He wrapped his arms around them. "We're missing a family member. Let's sit and figure out how to find your brother. I'm leaving for Missouri as soon as we're finished here. I'll track down that attorney, Alex Thomas, who handled the adoptions."

"I'll check the Missouri papers for birth announcements from twenty years ago," Adam volunteered.

Tye nodded, "Good idea. Your grandpa said the family was wealthy. Maybe the local newspaper made a big deal of the boy's addition to the family."

Jamie added, "I've checked adoption registries, but I'll check again more methodically."

"The next time you take off, may I go with you?" Adam inquired.

"We'll do it," Tye agreed.

Jamie questioned, "Have you considered writing about the search for your brother?"

"Would you mind? Your pregnancy is part of the story."

"I know a writer tells the whole story."

"That's great." The light caught the gleam in Adam's eyes. "Tye, will you take notes on your trip?"

"Absolutely. Time to get on the road. I hope to arrive in Missouri by midnight." Tye squeezed Adam's shoulder and gave Jamie a quick kiss. A smile stretched across his face as he went out the door.

Chapter Three

Lexie sat on the library's front steps as she called the Cherokee Nation Marshal Service. The August air surrounded her in a cocoon of heat. Petunias that bordered the sidewalk hung their heads as if praying for rain. Roots from the tree that gave her a little shade pierced through the earth reaching for a drop of rain that wasn't coming. Her eyes scanned up and down Main Street. Patches of brown marred every green plot. Each building was a different kind of stone or lumber from the red bricks of the library, down a block to the brown rock of her office down a block on the other side of the street. A voice finally answered her call.

"Larry Prather, please."

"I'm Marshal Prather."

"This is Lexie. I'm seeking information related to Chadwick Hawk's murder— fifteen years ago."

"That's mighty old and cold, Lexie. Not in your jurisdiction, either."

"I'm aware of that. However, my father's murder was two weeks before that event, which is in my jurisdiction. I'm speculating that the man who murdered Hawk killed my father."

"Perhaps a case too personal for you to see the truth even if it ran into you." Prather's words stung through the receiver.

"Don't worry. I see quite well. Is the person who investigated Hawk's case still around?"

"According to the computer case sheet, Gus Farmer was twenty-seven when he caught the case."

"Is he on duty?"

"Yep, but I'm not sure the Nation will release confidential information to a white girl."

"I'm as much Cherokee as you are, Prather."

"If you aren't living it girl, you're not part of it."

"Says the boy who isn't living it either," Lexie conveyed her words with as much acid as possible.

She certainly wouldn't admit it to Prather, but he had a point. She'd separated herself from her Cherokee heritage. Her dad took her to powwows when she was a kid, but when she became a teenager, she only listened to rock and country.

She knew Prather from high school. Their senior year he had a crush on her, then he suddenly resorted to vindictive gossip against her. She didn't know why and didn't care at the time. Now she worried that his attitude might hamper her investigation.

She dusted off her dirty derriere and headed for the blue and gray patrol car. Her blue slacks with a gray stripe down each leg, and blue shirt with gray buttons and collar matched the patrol car. Even though these colors were selected years before she became sheriff, she faced occasional teasing about the girlie endeavor of color coordinating the sheriff's department. When confronted, she assured her harassers that she considered changing everything to pink. Being the first female sheriff of Diffee resulted in a variety of gender jokes that she quickly learned to ignore.

The buzzing of her cell phone didn't slow her pace. One hand grabbed the door handle while the other one flipped open the phone. "Sheriff Wolfe here."

The words screeched into Lexie's ear, "You're needed at the office right now."

"Give me five minutes." *No point in asking questions over the phone.*

Emotional eruption wasn't Delia's usual reaction. She held the secretary and dispatcher position at the sheriff's office for thirty of her sixty-three years. Over the years she'd learned to face everything with calmness with the exception of the current call. *Wonder why today is different?*

Chapter Four

Delia's broad body stood framed in the doorway, as Lexie parked the cruiser beside the curb.

"Thank God, you're here," Delia spit out the words. Tresses of thin gray hair puffed from her bun, and one escaped strand hung to her shoulder.

Two other women occupied the office with Delia and the young deputy, Clay. He showed no inclination toward usefulness. Lexie wondered if he was hung over from the night before, but then traced his stare to the pretty blonde.

Lexie rolled her chair to a six-foot table, then directed Clay to get chairs for the two women.

She knew the blonde. Myrna Easton was a caseworker for the Department of Human Services in Diffee. The older woman with the pointy nose and auburn-streaked hair looked familiar.

"What's going on, Myrna?"

Her voice trembled, "Seth and Gabriel are gone."

Lexie knew the boys well. They were placed in DHS custody after Wilbur Langley left them alone in his drug house. The five- and two-year-old boys were the sons of Wilbur's live-in girlfriend.

The woman tugged her pointy nose. "That crazy woman would've killed me if I refused to let them go with her. She waved that gun and said she was goin' blow out both my eyes."

Lexie interrupted, "Your name?"

"I'm Paula Smithy, their foster mom. I get paid a little for taking in kids, but not enough to put up with loony shit."

"Who was behind the gun?" Clay asked Paula while patting Myrna's hand.

"Don't know her. She was skinny as a rail with raccoon eyes. I'd swear there was a golden hue around her mouth."

"Sounds like Naomi, their mother," Myrna offered.

Lexie agreed, "Huffers particularly like gold spray paint for their highs."

Paula squeezed her hands together. "I let her take them. What else could I do?"

"Nothing else," Lexie assured her. "You may go now, Ms. Smithy. I'll phone if I have questions. Give your contact information to Delia."

Clay put a reassuring hand on Myrna's shoulder. Lexie didn't miss the young woman reaching to press her hand over his. So her curly headed deputy had a girlfriend, and she'd completely missed it. Likely went to school together—both in their mid-twenties. *Myrna probably didn't have a clue that her love interest was a habitual drunk with lousy work ethics, not to mention his father, the Diffee mayor, who covered up all the guy's crap.*

"Myrna, return to work. I'll phone you as soon as I find the boys. Delia, you hold down the fort while Clay and I track down Naomi."

Delia swirled the loose strand of hair around her finger. "Those dear little boys deserved a good family, and they ended up with huffers and druggies."

"We'll get them," Clay assured Delia as he walked Myrna to the door.

"Let's get going," Lexie directed. "We'll hitch a trailer to the patrol car and pick up ATVs."

Chapter Five

An hour later the pair pulled up beside Lulu's Country Store and Diner. Lexie opened the restaurant door and stuck her head in, "Lulu, okay if we park the patrol car here?"

The little lady sauntered from the kitchen. The smell of grease assaulted Lexie's nose as Lulu hugged her. "I heard you turned eighty?"

"That's a true story," Lulu's floured hands swiped her plaid apron. "I expect I'll retire in another ten years. Best not to overdo, you know. Used to be six feet, but now I've shrunk to five cause of this here restaurant work."

Lexie's laughter joined with Lulu's. "We'll return in two or three hours."

"No hurry."

Lexie straddled the ATV, then pulled in front of Clay. Neither spoke as Lexie maneuvered a path over the solid earth and between trees toward Wilbur's house in the woods.

The ache in her chest might have made others fear a heart attack was about to strike, but Lexie knew her pain was emotional, not physical. This was the first time she'd visited these woods since she killed Toby. He shot Wilbur in the arm, then threatened to do worse. Taking Toby's life left a void inside her—an empty hole.

Within a mile of Wilbur's place, they left the noisy machines behind. They trudged through the rocky terrain toward the broken down shack.

A rust-speckled '57 Ford was parked in the front yard, and two flea-ridden dogs barked ferociously. Their bones were visible under thin layers of spotted fur. Not possessing enough willpower to attack the intruders, they soon laid down under a tree.

She signaled Clay to the back yard. Lexie pounded the front door.

"Naomi, open the door. It's the Sheriff," Lexie shouted.

The chain lock rattled and the door opened slowly. Seth's blood-smudged face peeked out.

Lexie eased the screen open. The five-year-old wrapped his arms around her waist. His face pushed against her stomach. She bent to hold him. A bloody film of moisture formed on the side of her neck from his tears. In the background, she heard Gabriel crying. *The boys are alive, but where is Naomi?*

Clay's face was a pallid caricature of horror as he turned from the bedroom door toward Lexie. "Their mother's in there."

She pushed the door back. Gabriel's head rested on his dead mother's chest. Naomi's belly area was a mush of blood and flesh blown out from a shotgun blast.

Lexie picked Gabriel up and circled his small body in her arms. His wails filled the room as he clutched her.

Seth sat motionless on the sofa beside Clay. His little chin quivered as he bit his bottom lip.

"Clay, have Myrna meet us at Lulu's. Also, tell her the boys look okay physically, but need to be examined at the hospital as a precaution."

Lexie pulled a food-stained dishrag from a drawer and wiped the blood off their faces and hands. *They must have tried to help their mother or hug her after she was shot.*

Lexie placed Seth on the ATV in front of her and Gabriel went with Clay. It was a bumpy trip, one most children would've found glee in, but the boys made no sounds.

When the children were safe with Myrna and Clay was sent back to town, Lexie climbed back on the ATV. Soon state troopers would arrive to carry out the crime scene investigation.

Chapter Six

Tye threw his bag on the worn recliner then stretched out on the bed. The motel room was a smelly mixture of smoke and disinfectant with a couple of other unidentifiable odors that were best left unknown.

Tomorrow he'd put on his deputy uniform and pretend he was in the vicinity on sheriff business. His cover was a search for a Diffee fugitive that looked like the boy of whom he happened to have a photo on his cell phone—Adam. He didn't know if his sons were identical, but if they were, the search would be easier.

The plans in his head finally gave way to snoring, and he slept soundly in spite of the odors.

Morning brought a sunny day and a man intent on seeing his hope manifested into a lost son. His first stop was the sheriff's office in Canary, Missouri. Unlike the Diffee office, this one had new paint, shiny computers, and furniture that looked like grimy criminals weren't allowed to touch, much less sit there.

"I'm Deputy Alberta Crane, Ally for short." The woman stood and reached out a prosthetic arm. "Sorry, sometimes I forget to shake with my left hand. Tends to freak out small children and delicate females."

"Looks mighty handy. But you got nothing on me, lady." He pulled up his pants leg and revealed the metal pole that served as his right leg.

"A man with a fancy leg. Impressive."

"A gift of war, and yours?"

"Mine was the result of a thief with a poor shot. He actually aimed at my heart and missed."

"My favorite criminals, those who can't shoot straight. By the way, I'm Tye Wolfe, Deputy Sheriff from Diffee, Oklahoma."

"Well, what can I do for you, Fancy Leg?"

"I'm looking for this young man. He's accused of robbery in Diffee. I plan to bring him home to serve his time." Tye held his phone near Crane's bespectacled face.

"Doesn't look familiar. Give me his name and I'll look him up."

"No name, only a photo," Tye responded. "He was last seen with an attorney named Alex Thomas."

"I know Thomas. He retired from lawyering here years ago. Apparently he accumulated enough money off me, and the rest of the divorcees in town to take early retirement."

"Any family?" Tye questioned.

"Just a son, probably about five years old when Thomas left town."

"Son?" Tye's heart raced inside his chest.

"Story was that he adopted the boy."

A film of sweat formed on Tye's forehead. "Do you remember his son's name?"

Alberta stared at his moist face. "Only around the kid twice, that was when I tracked down Thomas to get his side of the story."

Tye stammered, "Side of what story?"

"If someone pissed Thomas off, he turned into a human explosive. He called names and threatened shit. There was always someone filing charges against him. He finally got tired of dealing with us and moved."

"To where?" Tye pushed back his hope.

"I don't generally pay attention to where hotheads go. I just add a thank you to my Sunday prayer, but Thomas was on probation, and there was no choice."

After five minutes on the computer, Ally came up with a rural address in Nevel, Kansas. Suspicion seeped into her words, "Why do you want Thomas' address?"

"Thomas' boy may be the one I'm looking for."

She shook her head, "This address is fifteen years old. Don't expect him to still live there. Why are you really looking for this kid?"

"He may be my lost son." Tye gave a "thanks" and headed for the door before Ally asked questions.

She called after him, "By the way, 'Boy' was all I ever heard Thomas call his kid."

What luck—to find an address this fast. The attorney either made up the story about a wealthy family adopting my son, or the people changed their minds and Thomas kept him. 'Boy'—a strange thing to call your son.

The cell phone buzz startled him as he peered at the Kansas map he'd purchased at Quick Stop. "Sheriff Wolfe, why are you bugging me on my day off?"

"I need you here—murder case."

"Who?"

"Gabriel and Seth's mom, Naomi. The boys were with her when she was shot—broken hearted little guys. Seth won't talk. Anyway, we're shorthanded and now this investigation. I'm sorry, I know how important your search is, but I can't do without you."

"I'll make a stop in Nevel, Kansas, but I'll get home for the night shift tomorrow," Tye promised.

"My friend Sloan is the sheriff in Nevel. Remember, I told you about him: early sixties, short, stout, military background."

"Sure, I remember. I'll see you tomorrow."

Chapter Seven

The sun peeked through the clouds as Tye entered the Nevel Sheriff's office. This place reminded him of his Diffee office. Nothing matched and the furnishings looked at least twenty-years-old. A week's worth of dust was accumulated on the desk that Sloan sat behind.

Sloan stood as if at attention. Tye curtailed the urge to salute. "I'm Tye Wolfe, brother of Sheriff Lexie Wolfe."

Sloan grasped his hand like a vise. "Sit down, son. That sister of yours solved my murder case. Ugly deal, that guy, Bud, who murdered all those women."

Tye agreed, "terrible situation."

"How can I help you, son?"

"I'm looking for a man named Alex Thomas, an attorney from Canary, Missouri. He left there because of trouble with the law. Deputy Alberta Crane told me that Thomas moved to Nevel." Tye handed him the address.

"This is about sixteen miles outside of town, a desolate area with old farm houses. What's your purpose?"

To lie or not to lie. Tye had a feeling Sloan would see through any fabrication. He decided the truth was the best route. Since Lexie helped Sloan, maybe he'd cooperate.

"Thomas may have ended up with my missing son. He claimed he was handling the adoption for someone else, but a son mysteriously showed up in his life. I want to know if my boy is okay."

Sloan rose from his chair, "I'll drive."

After a mile, Sloan started Viet Nam war stories. Time went quickly as Tye mentally compared Sloan's war experience to his own in Iraq.

On the drive, flat farmland extended for miles in every direction. It collided with the sky on the horizon.

"The world is flat after all," Tye joked.

Sloan chuckled, "Columbus didn't make it to Kansas or he'd never have spread that rumor about the world being round."

Their merged laughter filled the vehicle.

"There it is," Sloan pointed east, "it looks close, but we have miles to go."

Finally, the pavement curved into a rough road. Rocks spewed in all directions. Sloan stopped in front of Thomas' place.

The roof over the porch had fallen, leaving a shingled slide to the ground. Holly bushes snarled around the front steps. Weeds invaded the edges of rocks that once served as a walkway to the front porch.

The windows were broken. Each appeared to have suffered the blow of a large rock hurled from a strong arm. Even the birds didn't come close. The hope drained from Tye: nothing to sing about around here.

The men bypassed the buried front door and headed for the back. Sloan hollered as he pounded on the door. Tye heard the door trim cracking in response to Sloan's fist.

"Get the flashlight out of the truck, Tye. Soon it will be dark and it's probably already a dungeon in there."

Tye jogged to and from his assigned task.

Lines of sweat rippled down Sloan's red neck. "Let's hit this door together, but not too hard. If the door gives out, we'll fall flat on our faces."

"I hear you," Tye agreed.

One firm push and the door broke into three pieces as it fell into the interior. The first bedroom held a twin bed. A deteriorated Michael Jordan poster hung on the wall. The second bedroom held a full-sized bed and shelf after shelf of law books that reached the ceiling. The house was small: two bedrooms, one bathroom, a living area, and a kitchen. Dishes filled the drainer, and a dusty cloth covered the table. Towels hung on the bathroom bars. It was as if the inhabitants were snatched from existence. The house was a victim of weather and human neglect.

Thomas' name was written inside law books and on bills decaying on the old desk tucked in the corner. His son's name wasn't on anything in the smaller room. A door led from the kitchen to the basement.

The men walked gingerly down the rickety steps. On the bottom step, Sloan's body ricocheted. His hand flew into the air. "STOP!"

The urgency in Sloan's voice sent a chill through Tye. "What is it?"

"MURDER!"

Tye's foot touched the next step.

"Don't get in the crime area," Sloan ordered.

Tye stopped, but he clearly saw the skeleton with the bashed-in skull. His legs turned to mush and he lowered himself to seating. *Was this his son? Bones on a cement floor?*

"It's a male skeleton," Sloan reported to the person on the other end of his police radio. "Bring the team and get here ASAP."

He turned to Tye. "Go outside. I can't have you involved in this investigation."

"It may be my son."

"I know, but keep hope for now."

Tye pulled himself from the step with a tug from Sloan's muscular arm.

Outside, Tye sank into the grass that had deteriorated to straw under the Kansas sun. His fingers pressed the rough surface. Dark had fallen, a fact he appreciated. Tears accumulated in the circles under his eyes then escaped down his nose. Perhaps he'd lost the son that he never knew. A son who lived in a house with a basement equipped like a torture chamber.

Powerful lights, brought by Sloan's deputy, lit up the house's interior as if the sun was captured inside.

Sloan walked forward, steps precise, his frame straight. Tye stood. The sheriff pulled out plastic gloves and stretched them over his stubby fingers. He signaled Tye to open his mouth, then swabbed the inside of his cheek.

"Deputy Baker will drive you back to your vehicle. As soon as I run the DNA samples, we'll find out if you're a match for the victim."

Tye nodded his head in understanding.

"Go home, son. You can't do anything here."

Tye looked back twice. The light shone from the basement window into the eerie darkness of the night.

Baker and he didn't exchange a word until they reached Tye's vehicle at the sheriff's office.

"I'll pray for you," Baker stated.

Tye's feet dragged across the pavement which moved his slouched frame toward his truck.

Chapter Eight

Lexie spoke into her cell phone, "Delia, I'll stop at Paula Smithy's house to visit Seth. I'll question Farmer at Cherokee Nation after I leave Seth. Is everything okay there?"

"Yes," Delia's voice lowered, "with the exception that Clay's asleep on his desk."

Irritation seeped into Lexie's words, "Still drunk or a hangover?"

"Not sure."

"I'll return in a couple of hours. If he wakes before then, tell him to stay put."

"I will, goodbye."

Lexie stopped the patrol car in front of Paula's house. The two-story looked like a brick square. No awnings or shutters decorated the exterior. Block steps led to a small porch. The sound of crying echoed from the other side of the door.

Paula's hair was matted and stuck out on one side. Swollen, red bags underscored her eyes. "Come in, Lexie—sorry so slow to reach the door. Up all night with Gabriel and I can't get Seth to eat anything. Thank goodness my daycare is closed on Saturday or I'd tear out my hair."

"Don't apologize. I know you have your hands full. I'll visit with Seth outside for a few minutes."

"Good luck, I can't get the poor child to utter a word." Paula wrapped an egg biscuit in a napkin. "Here, take this—maybe he'll eat for you."

Seth's body slumped against the wall, his spirit crushed by the weight of his mother's murder.

"Seth," Lexie coaxed, "we'll talk outside where Gabriel can't hear us."

His body stayed anchored against the wall.

"I need your help," Lexie stated flatly.

His footsteps moved slowly toward her. Her comforting arm wrapped around his shoulders as they walked outside.

"Let's sit on that bench in front of the big tree."

Seth's eyes focused on the ground while he followed her.

"Do you remember my friend Red? He took you up in his airplane. He plans to train you as his co-pilot, when you're older."

Seth nodded as his eyes focused on the ground.

"Clay, my curly-headed deputy, was on the plane that day, too. And someone else was there. Who was that?"

"Tye," a low voice muttered.

"That's right—my brother, Tye."

Seth nodded, then sat beside her on the bench.

Lexie pressed her hand over his. "You're only five, but I know you've taken care of Gabriel all his life. I don't want to ask him questions about who murdered your mama, but if you won't tell me, I'll ask him."

The small head moved from side to side.

"Tye and I are like you and Gabriel. Someone murdered our father long ago. The bad guy got away."

Seth whimpered, "Are you sad?"

"Yes," Lexie answered softly, "but I will catch the killer someday and he will go to jail for the rest of his life."

"I see Mama in my head."

"Yes," Lexie circled her arm closely around him. "My dad is in my head, too. He was hurt bad, just like your mama. Who shot your mama, Seth?"

Anger sparked his words, "Toby's kin slammed a cane into Mama's head and then shot her."

"A woman?"

"Don't know her name."

"What did she say to your mama?"

Seth's gaze lifted to Lexie's eyes. "That Toby was dead because of her old man. That Wilbur stole Toby's money and the sheriff shot him dead."

Seth didn't know that she was the sheriff who shot Toby. "Was the woman tall, short, fat, or skinny?"

"She was fat like a hippo, with a man mustache. Her nose got lost in her mush face. Looked like a golden ring around her mouth."

Lexie squeezed his hand. This was probably the best description she'd ever gotten from a witness. "Why didn't the woman hurt you and Gabriel?"

"Mama hid us in the closet when the woman yelled outside the front door."

"How did you see her?"

"Through a gunshot hole in the closet door."

The hole was a leftover from her shoot-out with Toby. "Gabriel didn't see your mama get shot?"

"No."

"Seth, you did good. I have one more job for you. Eat this egg biscuit so you can stay strong and help with this case." She kept him in the crook of her arm as he nibbled on his breakfast.

"Is there anything I can do for you, Seth?" She thought he'd ask her to find his mother's killer.

"Would Tye come see me?"

"He's in Kansas today, but as soon as he gets home, I'll tell him to stop by. I know he'd like to see you."

Lexie walked the sad-eyed boy back to Paula. "He liked that egg biscuit."

"Praise the Lord, the boy has some food in him."

Lexie patted Gabriel's head and gave Seth an unreturned hug, "See you soon."

Chapter Nine

Her drive to the Cherokee Marshal Service was a short one. She hoped Larry Prather would be out on a case—no such luck. The former wrestler was seated in the reception area.

"What took so long, Wolfe? Did you stop and pretty up before you came? Better still, did you decide to keep your nose out of our cases?"

Lexie fired back, "Unlike you, Prather, I wasn't sitting on my ass in a lobby. I was investigating a murder."

"You talkin' about that hooker-huffer Naomi?"

"I'm sure you have more knowledge of her professional favors than myself," Lexie smirked.

Larry's pocked skin reddened.

"I'm here to see Gus Farmer," Lexie directed her statement to the receptionist.

Prather commanded, "Follow me."

Gus Farmer was a full-blooded Cherokee in his mid-forties and easy on the eyes. He stood when she entered.

"Have a seat, Sheriff Wolfe."

Prather slouched on the chair beside her.

"Larry said you wanted information about Hawk."

"Yes. When I examined old newspapers, I discovered he was murdered a few days after my father."

"I remember that case well, mainly because I failed my first murder investigation. Why do you think the killings are connected?"

"Both were Cherokee men who participated in competitive dance. Also, they were murdered within the same time frame."

"Was your father killed with an arrow?"

"No similarity there: my father was stabbed, as was I." Lexie touched the right side of her face to prove her point.

Farmer's voice erupted, "I forgot you were there."

"I was sixteen at the time. The killer's head and face were completely covered by a sock hat. Frankly, my brain blocked out much of that day."

"I can understand that," Farmer's eyes conveyed sympathy.

Prather's laugh vibrated the paper in his hand. "The sheriff is a lousy murder witness."

Farmer's words shot toward Prather, "Don't be a jerk."

Lexie changed the subject as quickly as the sentence could get out of her mouth. Male-pissing matches weren't entertaining. "The newspaper said you apprehended a suspect: Leroy Grass."

"Locked him up twenty-four hours. Grass and Hawk fought at a powwow a few days before the murder. Story was that Hawk cheated on Leroy's daughter."

"Why was he released?"

"Leroy's daughter swore that Grass was with her and his sick mother at the hospital. His mom corroborated the story and so did a nurse."

"You completely ruled him out?"

"No, however, back then we didn't have the technology to pinpoint the time of death within a short period. It wouldn't have helped anyway, because the nurse was vague about what time Grass was actually at the hospital."

Lexie scooted forward, "Do you think he's innocent?"

Farmer shrugged and leaned back. "I don't know. Leroy was the only suspect at the time, but that doesn't make him guilty."

"Where is he now?"

"Lives out in the woods with three pit bulls, a big shotgun, and probably a bow."

Prather piped in, "Don't mess with Leroy, little sheriff."

Lexie sniped, "How sweet, Prather, you're worried about my well-being."

"I'm concerned you won't keep your nose out of Cherokee business."

"Surely you don't think I'd dare cross horns with you." She turned to Farmer as she exited, "Thanks for the information."

"You're welcome."

Lexie heard the men's comments when she paused outside the door.

"Damn you, Farmer. You'd sell out the Nation to get on the good side of a pretty woman."

"Better than being an asshole."

Lexie barely reached the corner before Prather stormed out the door.

Chapter Ten

"Jamie, call Adam and ask him to meet me at your place in an hour."

"What did you find out?"

"I'll tell you when I get there." He pushed the off button to stop the next question.

Tye hadn't eaten or slept since yesterday. His body was on alert all night, waiting for a phone call that wouldn't come for days or even weeks. *Sloan was a good guy. He'd hurry up the DNA process.*

His Kansas trip ended when he stopped in front of Jamie's duplex. Adam's truck was already there. He found them at the kitchen table. Jamie's face searched his as he sank into a chair.

Adam didn't sense the dread in the air. He quickly talked about his Missouri newspaper search. "I looked through all the birth announcements in Canary and the surrounding towns. Nothing gave a clue as to where my brother ended up."

"I'm still working on the adoption website," Jamie added. She noted the tremor in Tye's right hand, "What's wrong?"

"You can both stop looking," Tye mumbled.

Adam's words whooped out, "You found him?"

"Maybe, won't know until I get a report back."

"What's wrong, Tye?" Jamie's question was little more than a whisper.

Tye stumbled over the words, "That attorney kept our son. I don't know why. I tracked them to Nevel, Kansas. The trail ended at a run-down house in the middle of nowhere. Sheriff Sloan entered the house with me. We found a male skeleton in the basement."

"Oh, no," Jamie wiped her emerging tears, then blew her nose on a napkin.

"You think it was my brother?"

"I don't know," Tye's voice cracked, "Sloan took a DNA sample from me. In a few days or weeks, I'll get word if our son was murdered in that basement."

Jamie's eyes bulged, "Murdered?"

"There was a strong blow to the victim's head."

Adam cleared his throat, "What now?"

"Nothing to do but wait. We'll eventually bring him home; to live or to bury."

Jamie's chair sent a squeal into the air as she pushed back from the table. Her running feet banged against the wood floor. Then Tye heard a slam, the bed squeak, and uncontrollable sobs from the other side of the door.

"Go home, son. I'll stay with Jamie."

Chapter Eleven

Lexie found Clay sprawled across his desk, just as Delia described over the phone.

She hollered a foot from his right ear, "Wake up deputy!"

Clay startled like an animal caught off guard. His greasy blond hair almost covered his blue eyes. Lexie moved back a few feet to escape the pungent odor that surrounded him.

"Delia, will you order lunch across the street? Clay and I need alone time."

"Sure, sure." Delia maneuvered herself from the stool in front of the computer, grabbed her purse, and scurried out the door.

Lexie suppressed the urge to yell. "What's going on with you, Clay? I know you have a drinking problem, but the last couple of months it has gotten out of control. I can't rely on you."

"It's personal stuff. I'll straighten up."

"If you show up drunk again, you're fired. Do you understand?"

"I hear you," he snarled, "I told you I'd straighten up. You better remember that my dad, the mayor, will have a word or two to say about any firing."

His words ended her resolve to stay calm. "Quit hiding behind your father and grow up."

Clay struggled from the chair and sped toward the door. Once he grabbed a chair back to maintain his balance.

Lexie wandered around the office, so hyped from anger she couldn't sit still. She smelled the roses on Delia's desk. Her finger flicked peeling, gray paint from the deteriorating wall surface. She counted the metal file cabinets in Spanish. If and when the county allotted money, she planned to paint the depressing walls, find file cabinets that matched, and buy a new computer.

Finally, she sat down and twisted her braid into a knot on her head. *If only Tye would show up so they could discuss Clay, Naomi's murder, and Leroy Grass.* As if wishes came true, the door opened and there he was.

He lumbered across the room. Lexie knew he was exhausted by the way he dragged his fake leg. "You look like the world ended and you were in the last battle."

"Part of my world may have ended."

"Your son?"

"I traced him to an old house in Sloan's jurisdiction. A skeleton with a smashed-in skull and a variety of torture devices were in the basement."

"Dear God, you think it's him?"

"That's the nightmare that won't end until the DNA results come back."

"I'm so sorry. How is Jamie holding up?"

"She fell apart. Blames herself for giving up the boys. Let's talk about something else."

"Seth asked you to come see him. He must have really 'taken a shine to you,' as Grandpa used to say."

"That's strange."

"Oh, I don't think it's that surprising. You're both strong, silent types. His spirit was broken. I told him about our dad's murder to give him some kinship with us."

"Sounds like a good idea. I'll visit him the first chance I get."

"I'd like backup at Toby's place when I apprehend Naomi's murderer. I came up with the name based on Seth's description. She's Wanda Carpenter, Toby's common-law wife. We have prints and hair from the crime scene. It's an easy solve."

"Red flying us?"

"He'll meet us at the airfield in ninety minutes." Lexie rescued Delia as she came in the door with food bags clutched in both hands.

Delia squeezed Tye's shoulder when she recognized the sadness in his eyes.

"There's my lady," he said, and managed to give her a fake smile.

"I saw your truck out front, so I added to the order."

"You're always right on cue, Delia," Lexie divided up the food.

"I try, but my brain occasionally has farts and I miss things."

Tye's smile was genuine, "Brain farts. Hey, I'll remember that excuse the next time I screw up."

Chapter Twelve

On the way to the airfield which was actually a pasture, Lexie gave Tye updates on their father's killer as well as Clay's drunken state.

Red leaned against the side of his Cessna and watched as they walked toward him. "Hi, beautiful!"

Tye responded, "Hello, gorgeous!"

"Very funny, man," Red shook Tye's hand, then pulled Lexie to his chest. He gave her a quick smooch on the lips.

"I'm on duty, Red Anderson. Stop that kissing."

"But you're irresistible!" Red wrapped an arm around her shoulder and guided her to the plane.

Tye climbed into the plane first. Red took the opportunity and gave her another kiss.

"Too much public display of affection," Lexie quipped.

"Never," was Red's response. After he settled into the pilot's seat, he cocked his head back. "Where are we going?"

"Toby and Wanda lived out in the woods, or as Grandpa used to say, 'in the middle of nowhere.' Drop us off a few miles north of Wilbur's place and we'll hike in."

"The trees have everything camouflaged, so it'll be difficult to find a landing site. Toby didn't want anyone to know where his drug business was hidden."

Miles later, Tye pointed out the window, "I'd swear that's an antennae."

"Damn good eyes," Red acknowledged.

Lexie sighed, "Not such a search, after all."

"No parachutes required," Red commented, "I see a clearing. You won't hike over two miles."

The plane veered from side-to-side as it made contact with the rough terrain. The wood benches, that Red installed to accommodate parachute jumpers, vibrated. The plane stopped suddenly.

"I'd like to go along," Red volunteered.

"Wouldn't hurt," Tye agreed. "Sometimes there are six or eight gun-toting loonies in these drug families."

Red pulled his rifle from under the seat. "I'll bring this so I'll look ominous."

Lexie's head shook, "Don't use it unless it's life or death."

The scorching summer left them a dry creek bed that served as their path through the trees.

Tye's body lurched forward when small stones rolled under his feet, leaving him unsteady as he moved forward. A day and a half since he slept, exhaustion took its toll. Sixty yards from the house a shot rang out, then another, and another. Startled, he dropped to the ground.

Lexie and Red took cover in the bushes that formed a border around the wire and post fence. Heavy footsteps pounded the earth. She watched as Wanda tromped toward Tye. A shotgun barrel perched on her shoulder pointed toward the sky. Combat boots with big toes protruding through the split leather stopped at Tye. Lexie pulled her gun from the holster and crept forward.

Wanda hollered, "What you doin' on my place?"

Humor mingled in Tye's words, "Looking for a murderess."

Wanda's words hissed between toothless gums, "Funny guy, is ya?"

"Occasionally."

"You best get out of here, fool. My man is gettin' home soon."

"Well, Wanda, it'll take a while. It's a long trip from Hell to Diffee."

"You son-of-a-bitch. I is goin' splatter your guts all over these here woods."

"Think about it, Wanda. There was no witness to Naomi's murder. What the hell, you may even go free. But if you kill me, the sheriff and deputy hidden in the bushes will witness you into the electric chair. You'll light up like the White House Christmas tree."

"You're a lyin' Injun."

He grabbed and twisted Wanda's shotgun as he plowed his body into her. She pulled the trigger on her downward spiral. A bullet sang above their heads, then splintered the bark of a tree a few yards away. Wanda smashed into the earth's floor and moaned. She looked straight into Lexie's eyes.

"Howdy, Wanda! No time for a nap."

"Leave, bitch! You killed my man!"

"He was caught shooting an unarmed man," Lexie responded.

"That's crap. Wilbur ain't no man. He's a money-stealing horse's ass, just like his whore, Naomi."

"Naomi is why I'm here. Wanda Carpenter, you're under arrest for the murder of Naomi Sims."

Tye knelt beside the fallen woman while he recited her rights.

"Get away from me, asshole. I's hurt. Can't get up."

Red placed his hands under her armpits and pushed her to sitting. Then Tye lifted one side while Red handled the other. Together they got her to a wobbly standing position.

"I ain't goin' nowhere."

"Either you walk or we drag you," Lexie threatened.

"You got no witness. You got nothin' on me."

"Technology is a wonderful thing, Wanda. I have fingerprints from the murder scene that match yours on file for shoplifting. I bet I'll soon have a DNA match from the your spit that you'll so generously give me."

"Eureka," Tye called out, "there's blood on your cane that probably belonged to Naomi. This case is so tight you'll think you're trapped in a coon's cage."

Wanda's belligerent tone diminished to curtailed hatred, "I gotta tell my kin folks."

Lexie shook her head. "I'll pass on that experience today. I'll leave a note under this rock so they'll know you're in jail."

The thirty-minute trek back to the plane turned into two hours thanks to Wanda's attitude and pace. The flight back was filled with all things Wanda: cussing, sobbing, and odors that accumulated from weeks without showers.

Chapter Thirteen

Lexie sent her exhausted brother home and phoned Clay. Since he slept on his desk all day, she'd switch him back to night shift now instead of later.

When he arrived, Lexie gave him instructions on their new boarder.

"Wanda has a court appearance Monday. She already ate supper. Give her the snacks on my desk if she gets hungry. Tye will relieve you at 6 a.m."

Clay's response was a subdued, "Yeah."

After spouting the orders, Lexie hurried out the door. The summer night withheld air. Sweat beads erupted on her body. Her lungs labored to take in enough oxygen.

She flung the door of her duplex open and stripped off the uniform as she walked toward the shower. The cool water made streams down her body, and she splashed a handful on her face. Black panties and a sleeveless undershirt were her sleepers of choice. After crawling in bed, she pushed the old red quilt to the foot of the bed. Eventually, the top sheet ended up scrunched beside it.

She lay spread-eagle, staring at the ceiling. Her old air conditioner groaned in the background. Tomorrow she'd question Leroy Grass. Maybe get a close-up look at his shotgun and man-eating dogs.

At 4 a.m. she jerked awake. A vivid, pit bull nightmare, in which she was their rump roast, crept into her unconscious. Sleep refused to return. She cleaned out the refrigerator and vowed to purchase groceries instead of fast food.

After another cool shower, she put on blue jean cutoffs and a green, sleeveless pullover. No uniform today. She couldn't look official when she went to see Leroy on Cherokee land.

At 8 a.m. she slid the metal latch on Leroy's gate. A wire fence surrounded Leroy's place. No sign of Leroy or his ferocious pets. Every attempt was made to not disturb the quiet. She rounded the fallen branches in the yard, and was almost to the front steps before the little monster's sharp bark summoned the others to hightail around the corner of the house.

They surrounded her, unsure of where to take the first bite of the 125 pound visitor. Sharp teeth protruded from their growling mouths. One nipped at her tennis shoe. Her kick motivated him to move closer. A shot rang into the air and the trio scampered off, their Lexie breakfast left behind. *Was Leroy saving me or scaring me off?*

A man walked toward her, his rifle in the business position. At least a foot taller than Lexie's 5 feet 7 inch height, she raised her chin to make eye contact.

A gray braid touched each shoulder. His eyes were deep inside dark hollows, flesh pulled tight over his bones leaving no room for fat.

"What do you want?" he growled. *Perhaps he'd taken a lesson or two from his pets.*

Lexie gulped, "A conversation with you."

"I ain't got nothin' to say, woman."

"My name is Lexie Wolfe. My father, Nodin, was murdered years ago, and I'm looking for his killer."

Leroy lowered his shotgun. "That's got nothin' to do with me."

Lexie moved closer, "You were both Indian dancers. Did you hear rumors at a powwow?"

"You think I killed Hawk and your father?"

"It crossed my mind."

"Nodin was my friend. Hawk cheated on my daughter—dishonored my family. If I didn't kill him, I should have. The two men are opposites in my mind. I didn't kill your father."

"I know. You're much taller than the man I jumped on from behind."

"My height clears me?"

Disappointment crept into her one word reply, "Yes."

His eyes formed into slits. "You hoped I was a murderer?"

"You were my only clue, and now I have none."

"Don't you care if I killed Hawk?"

"That problem belongs to Cherokee Marshal Service."

"Don't come around here no more," Leroy warned, "them dogs will eat you for supper."

Lexie laughed, "I dreamed last night that they ate me for breakfast. So I'm feeling lucky today."

Leroy's stone face cracked a little. "I'll follow you to the gate."

"Thanks, don't want my nightmare to come true."

As her hand touched the car door handle, Leroy's words resonated in the wind behind her. "Trouble begins at home."

Lexie turned to ask what he meant, but his voice activated the canine corps, so she escaped to the safety of her Jeep.

Chapter Fourteen

Lexie stopped by home and changed into a white peasant blouse. She brushed her hair, pulled the sides back, then fastened it with a silver barrette. A little lip-gloss, brown eyeliner, and a touch of perfume finished her prep for a picnic with Red.

His sudden invitation, after the plane ride, took Lexie by surprise. Red never seemed like a picnic kind of guy. He even said he'd bring the lunch. All she had to do was show up at the shore of Turtle Creek near his old home place.

It was a perfect day, much deserved by the human race after the scorcher yesterday. September would soon arrive, but not soon enough as far as she was concerned.

Red was leaning against an oak tree when she arrived. Not his typical look today. His auburn hair was cut close to tame the natural curl. His blue plaid cowboy shirt and pressed blue jeans looked out of place on a hot day.

"You look mighty handsome, Cowboy."

"Ready to lasso my sweetheart."

He gave her a firm hug without the expected kiss.

Red pointed to an old, diamond patterned quilt he'd spread under a tree. She sank down onto its worn surface. She watched as he pulled their lunch out of a grocery bag. He opened the bread, squirted on some mustard and added a slice of cheese and bologna on each. A bag of potato chips and two peanut butter cookies completed the feast.

She ate while they watched the meandering water flow down the creek bed. Chewing sandwiches and chips substituted for conversation. The gentle breeze played with her hair. She pushed it back, and caught Red staring at her.

"You're sad today," he concluded.

"Sorry I'm a downer. I've come to a dead end in Dad's investigation."

His eyes studied her face. "I have a proposition for you."

"You always have a scheme, Red Anderson." She playfully pinched his cheek, hoping the closeness would inspire a kiss or two that he was so stingy with today.

"Marry me, Lexie."

"I've told you a dozen times that my first priority is to see my father's killer locked away forever, or fried in the electric chair. Until that day, you and that redheaded baby you want will have to wait."

"Obsessed by revenge, are you?"

"I prefer justice to revenge, but whichever it is, that's my life's purpose for now." Silence took over as Red processed his latest refusal. She figured he was angry at her continued rejection.

He pulled her toward his chest. "I have a proposition for you."

Lexie grumbled, "Same old story."

Red scowled, "Do you love me or is the case an excuse to put me off?"

She planted a kiss square on his lips. "I started loving you when I was a teenager. Remember how I crawled into bed with you that morning, when my family left early to fish? I was mad at you for months, because you rejected me after that one great kiss. Since then, no man could compete with you."

"So that's a yes." He caught her curious gaze. "Marrying me is the fastest way to solve your father's case."

"Give me a break, Red."

"Shut up and listen. If we get married sooner rather than later, we can invite back the people who were questioned after the murder. People you'd travel all over the U.S to interview. Isn't it better to have a reason to bring them to Diffee? I'd get my wife. You'd get a husband, and a room full of murder suspects."

The pair let nature sing its song. Lexie watched a woodpecker attack a tree. The beak made a rhythmic sound on the bark. The bird was like her, hammering away with no apparent results.

She felt a pressure release inside, a feeling she didn't recognize; something that was there as a child, but diminished to nothing after her father was murdered. The only word that came to mind was joy. *How did she deserve a man who was willing to merge their wedding with a murder investigation?*

She turned her face from the woodpecker to Red. His somber eyes studied her face, waiting for an answer.

Her lips locked on his and she kissed with all her might, then slowed to gentle kissing pecks on his forehead, cheeks, and chin, saying a quiet "yes" between each.

Red's laughter disturbed the woodpecker that cocked his head to identify the strange sound. The other birds chirped, either disturbed by the noise, or celebrating.

She rested her head on his chest and they lay wrapped in each other's arms for the next hour. The sound of his heart beating beneath her head confirmed her previous conclusion. *Yes, this is joy!*

"Come," he directed, "I have a surprise." He pulled her up, then held her hand as they walked toward his house on the hill.

The farmhouse, that was a deteriorated wreck the last time Lexie saw it, was newly painted a cream color with sage trim. The expanded front porch held a dark green swing and two wood rockers.

He held the front door open, "Come in, my lady."

No furniture, but the floors were all replaced with oak and the walls all painted a neutral shade. The kitchen housed all new chrome appliances and a table with six chairs.

"Where did you get these, Red? The carving on the chair backs is beautiful."

He pulled a knife from his pocket. "Just me and my handy helper."

"How did you finish all this work?"

"I worked and waited for years for the lady of the house. Tye helped me with the heavy lifting."

"I'm sorry. I've disappointed you so many times."

"That's all water under the bridge. This place is big enough for a wedding. I've imagined you walking down that curved staircase toward me."

Lexie nodded her head, "Perfect."

"We can get the place furnished and house our families for a few days. So what month, Lexie?"

"December, near Christmas, people coming in for the holidays won't have to make two trips."

"Good idea."

Lexie gave him a quick kiss. "I hate to say this, but I must relieve Tye at the office. I can't wait to tell him."

"Okay, my love." They walked to the vehicles hand in hand. Neither wanted to end their farewell embrace.

"I forgot." He pulled a small golden box out of his glove compartment. "For you."

Tears filled Lexie's eyes as she looked inside the box. A gold and silver twisted band with a single diamond moved from Red's hand to her finger. She didn't speak, but nature provided background music.

Chapter Fifteen

Lexie positioned her hand on the steering wheel so she'd see the ring at every opportunity. Twice she held it at eye level to get the full impact of its beauty.

She never admitted to herself how much she wanted a life with Red. Now she lamented all the years she wasted. *Hopefully, being a good wife will make up for his long wait.*

Tye was recording a traffic ticket when she arrived. Lexie held one hand inside the other.

"Hurt yourself?"

"I got a stone in my finger at the lake."

"Put your hand under the lamp. I'll dig it out," Tye offered.

She flattened her left hand on the desktop.

"You did it! You finally said, 'yes'!"

"I did!"

Tye jumped up and grabbed her hands. They hopped up and down like kids.

"Damn, took you forever. I thought you'd need a walker to get down the aisle at ninety-two."

"Very funny, Bro."

"What happened to your resolve to find Dad's killer first?"

"Red's idea made more sense. He said our wedding would put all the people, who were around during the murder, back into Diffee. I can re-interview them here instead of traveling to them."

"Doesn't sound like an activity a wedding planner will approve: a murder—matrimony mix."

Lexie's face grew taut, "Help me with something?"

"You certainly got serious all of a sudden."

"I have two months to get my ducks in a row. Every angle of Dad's case must be investigated before the wedding guests arrive."

Tye agreed, "Makes sense. What's my role?"

Lexie sat on the edge of his desk. "I'll tell you what I remember. You listen for discrepancies."

"I was in Iraq, so filling the void is your job."

"Ask me questions. Maybe something will arouse my memory."

"What's the first thing you recall from that day?"

"Mom yelled at me. She tried to force me to go shopping with her and Dixie."

"Mom always griped at you. Why does that stand out?"

"Because she was more cruel than usual. Told me I was a boy without a penis. Mom wanted to purchase feminine clothes for me because my appearance disgraced her. She tried to physically pull me from the recliner. At 5'2" and never doing anything to work up a sweat, she couldn't budge me. Called me a little bitch and went out the door."

Tye continued, "What else do you remember?"

"Guilt—I thought I was going to die, and my last interaction with her was defiance. When I awoke at the hospital, the first thing she said was that I got hurt because I was a disobedient brat."

Tye pushed the conversation back to the sequence of events. "Mom left after your argument?"

"Yes. I watched television until Dad came home. After I washed our lunch dishes, I propped myself against a pillow on my bed and read."

"Where was Dad?"

"Watching the noon news," Lexie answered.

"Was there a knock at the door?"

"I clearly remember a knock. You know how Mom always forgot her house keys. I figured she came home early to rant and rave about me to Dad. The voice I heard was male, so I continued reading."

"What did the voice say?"

"Just, 'Nodin.' Then there was a weird rasping noise and a crash, which was probably Dad hitting the floor."

"Then what?"

"I ran into the room. A man was leaning over Dad. Blood dripped from the knife in his hand. The guy raised the weapon to stab Dad again. I jumped on his back. He twirled around, slicing the side of my face with one swing. Then he smashed me against the wall. I was knocked out cold, based on what I heard later."

"Did the killer yell at you? Know your name?"

"He didn't say anything."

"Tell me about the man."

Lexie's tone was flat, "Average height, average build, and an average voice."

"How did he smell?"

Lexie's face brightened, "Maybe that's what my brain missed. He did have an odor."

"Good smell? Bad? Body odor?"

"He smelled fishy."

"TMAU."

"What are you talking about, Tye?"

"Trimethylaminuria, better known as fish odor syndrome."

Lexie's eyebrows lifted, "Since when do you know such a long word?"

"Don't insult me. I do know a few words that have more than four letters. Not sure I pronounced it right. Heard about it from Red."

"Red?"

"Years ago, he told me that some of his relatives have a genetic disorder that causes them to stink. He was afraid of inheriting it."

Lexie grasped her belly to steady the contents. "You'd think the man would've mentioned it to his wife to be."

"Since he didn't inherit TMAU, probably doesn't even think about it. But if he starts smelling like garbage, you'll have to adjust your menu."

"Thanks for the advice, Bro."

"Don't go around sniffing people, Lexie. If the killer watches what he eats, the smell may be eliminated. Who knows? Maybe the killer ate fried fish for lunch."

"You're just full of it today, and what you're full of isn't helpful."

"Sorry, Sis, but none of this stuff sounds relevant. We'll hope that someone is ready to speak up after all these years. If the murderer has died, others are more likely to release information since the fear of payback is off the table."

"I keep hoping I've blocked out something important; something my brain doesn't want acknowledged. Anyway, thanks for listening. I'll take over here until Clay arrives for late shift."

"Okay. I'll go see Seth on my way home."

"Good," Lexie answered.

Chapter Sixteen

"Come in, come in," Paula called from the interior of the house.

"It's Tye."

"Seth said you were coming to visit him. I told the boy I had no word of that and here you are." Paula yelled toward the bedroom, "Seth, come in here. You have a visitor."

The droopy-eyed child paused at the doorway.

"Get over here," Tye hunkered to a squatted position. It was Gabriel who took the opportunity to melt into his arms. "Seth, where's my hug?"

Seth came forward, arms straight, chin resting on his chest. Tye wrapped his arms around him, but it was like hugging a mini ironing board.

"Okay, guys, let's try out my new ball." He grabbed a boy with each hand and eased Seth forward while Gabriel tugged him toward the door.

Outside, he positioned the boys at the points of an imaginary triangle. Neither caught the ball, so Tye pulled the triangle in. Seth's frustration motivated him to switch the game to kick ball. Seth swung his leg forward with no luck, then hurled the ball toward Gabriel. Gabriel kicked the ball after a couple of licks. Tye attempted to trap the ball under one foot, but missed and fell flat on his butt.

The little guys looked down with rounded eyes.

"Good grief, can't you two help me up?"

A boy tugged at each arm. He pulled back and captured both of them in his lap. "Now you're trapped." He let the boys wiggle loose, then chased them around the yard.

Tye grabbed, then swung each boy in wide circles. "Now you're airplanes flying high!" After each flight, a boy fell to the ground in a giggly pile. He watched them a moment, smiling, then joined the pair on the ground. "This old plane engine needs gas."

Tye's cell phone vibrated in his pocket. A glance at the caller's name and a crushing feeling assaulted his chest. The rhythmic beating of his heart stalled. "Tye Wolfe here."

"It's Sloan."

"You got back to me sooner than I expected."

"I've developed a little clout in my forty-five years in law enforcement," Sloan bragged.

Tye placed a finger to his lips, signaling Gabriel to whisper. Seth was motionless beside him. Tye's apprehension escalated, "What are the results?"

"DNA proved that the victim was Alex Thomas."

Tye's held breath puffed into the phone, "You're sure?"

"Positive. No idea where your boy ended up, but he wasn't killed in that basement."

"Thanks for the quick results." The tension in Tye's chest eased.

"You're welcome. Got to get back to work. Good luck with your search."

Tye grabbed Seth and enveloped him in a hug with Gabriel.

"Happy?" Gabriel said as he wiggled free.

"Very happy. That man told me that my son is okay."

"You're his daddy?" Seth asked as he escaped from the hug. "I never had a daddy."

"I bet Myrna is looking for a daddy for you," Tye assured him.

Seth's expression was devoid of emotion.

Paula called from the porch, "Time to eat, guys. You're welcome to join us, Tye."

"I'll take a rain check, Paula. I'll visit again in a few days. Seth, you take care of that ball for us."

Gabriel returned his hug, but Seth only offered a weak wave.

Tye pressed speed dial on his phone as he walked toward his truck. Jamie answered on the first ring.

"Great news! The skeleton wasn't our son."

"Thank God!" she shrieked.

"I'll head to Kansas and pick up our son's trail as soon as I'm packed. I'll phone around 10 o'clock every night to give you updates."

"Have you told Adam?"

"Not yet, I'll ask if he wants to come."

"I love you, Tye."

"I love you, too. I'll stay in touch."

Next he punched in Adam's number. "I heard from Sloan. Your brother wasn't the victim in the basement. Are you ready to join the hunt? I'm packing a bag and leaving tonight."

"I'll meet you in an hour," Adam agreed.

Tye clicked his phone shut. His sorrow evaporated into hope. *Someday I'll meet my other son.*

Chapter Seventeen

Tye was gone again. His quick phone call the evening before relieved Lexie's fear about her nephew, which was a wonderful thing. However, Tye left her, Delia, and unreliable Clay to hold down the fort.

An idea popped into her head: ask Ruben to work part-time. He was the Sheriff of Diffee years ago. Now his primary activity—or lack of activity—was sitting on the bench outside Dixie's restaurant with Sam.

There was a double motive. Ruben was the sheriff who investigated her father's murder. He'd have invaluable case knowledge. Somehow, she'd camouflage the fact that she thought his investigation was half-assed.

As she drove her vehicle into a diagonal spot in front of her office, she glanced across the street. Ruben and his pal hadn't yet occupied their cement throne.

Delia arranged a new bouquet of flowers. Clay cleaned his gun. Wanda snored from the jail cot.

"Morning," Lexie said.

Clay echoed, "Morning."

"Good morning to you," Delia responded.

Lexie grinned, "I have good news and good news. The skeleton in the Kansas basement wasn't Tye's son."

Delia reached her hands toward heaven, "Praise the Lord."

Lexie rested her hand on her chest, "This is the second thing."

"My goodness, my goodness," Delia jumped from her chair and hugged Lexie, "It's beautiful!"

Clay's bored tone rang out, "Who gave it to you?"

"Red Anderson, of course," Delia blurted.

Wanda's tone bit, "I'm glad you folks are havin' such a fine time. I is starvin.' Where's my grub?"

Clay's eyes clamped on her, "You look like you'll survive."

"Zip it," Lexie snapped. "Here's a ten, buy Wanda the deluxe breakfast at Dixie's."

His feet shuffled across the floor.

"Fire that little shit." Wanda's words shot across the room in time for Clay to hear them as he exited.

"You have a point, Wanda," Lexie agreed.

After breakfast, Clay accompanied Wanda to the courthouse for her arraignment.

Chapter Eighteen

The trip, at first, was quiet. The father and son were barely acquainted. After a while, the flat plains left nothing to keep them awake, so chatter was their only recourse.

Tye started the conversation with tales of his Bogotá, Columbia trip. He told stories; one about a giant guide who called him "girl;" another about fallen leaves that marched along the forested floor on their own but, upon close scrutiny, he had discovered there were ants underneath that transported them in a long line.

Adam contributed stories of his early years with his adoptive parents. Eventually, he spoke about their deaths in a plane crash. "That's why I ended up in Diffee with my Grandpa Carr."

After the boy fell asleep, Tye lamented that Adam wasn't a boy anymore. Nineteen years of fathering gone, and who knew how many years he'd miss of his other son's life.

The Chevy Avalanche took the gravel curve into the motel lot with a series of bumps. Adam's head vibrated against the window. Red indentions marked where his head had pressed against the glass for the past hour from an unintended nap. He straightened his body. "Sorry, I wanted to help keep you awake and nodded off."

"All you missed was a coyote," Tye responded. "I'll check in the motel. We'll get a few hours sleep before we start our search."

"Sounds good to me." Adam grabbed the bags from the truck's second seat.

A couple of too firm beds, a john, and drapes to shut out the world were all they required. Soon Adam's snoring grew soft and gentle. Tye added an occasional snort to the night air.

It was 10 a.m. before they convinced each other it was time to shower, pack, and find some breakfast. The meal finished, they headed toward the house where Adam's brother lived.

The place was marked off as the investigation continued. The pair exited the truck. Sloan leaned against a maple tree. "Any information on my son?" Tye called.

"I'd say I was surprised to see you back here, but I'm not." Sloan shook Tye's hand.

"This is my son, Adam."

"Glad to meet you. A newspaper reporter?"

"Yes, sir. I try."

Sloan's eyes returned to Tye's face. "Back to your question. I traced the last name Thomas with the birthdate you gave me and came up with nothing. Kid must use a different last name."

"Thomas is a common name. It's like looking for a needle in a haystack," Tye added.

"State's interested in this case, probably because of all the newspaper coverage. Nothing like a mystery to get reporters excited, right Adam?"

"Yes sir, although law enforcement frequently doesn't care for our curiosity. Something Sheriff Lexie taught me by avoiding my questions."

Sloan drawled, "True indeed!"

Tye glanced at his watch. "We got to get moving. Any thoughts on where a young man might hang out in this county?"

"Not much around here. High school kids congregate around the Burger Station on Friday and Saturday nights. Older kids hit the two bars on First Street. A bar down by the pier is where the motorcycle guys hang out."

"We'll wander around town, and visit the barbershop, grocery store, gas stations and garages. Maybe someone will recognize Adam."

"Identical twins?"

"We don't know," Adam responded.

Sloan straightened to a military stance and saluted the pair. "Call me if you find anything."

"Will do," Tye assured him. "We'll leave late tonight, so won't see you again this visit."

"Good luck!"

Tye glanced back at the small house. He didn't allow himself thoughts of the horrors that basement revealed to Sloan.

Chapter Nineteen

"Delia, will you help plan my wedding?"

"Me?" Delia rolled her chair from the computer and looked at Lexie across the paper piles camouflaging her desk.

"There's no one I'd rather have assist me."

"Gosh, of course. We'll make to do lists over lunch. I dreamed of planning my own wedding, but my prince fizzled out."

"Who was that prince, Delia?"

"Not important, all ancient history."

"Cecil Lansbury?"

"Yep, that big, baby-faced attorney broke my heart. He asked me to marry him, then went gaga-eyed over another woman. She took him away from me, then dropped him like a hot pan. He begged forgiveness, but no way I wanted a man who was that fickle."

"Who was the woman?"

"Best to leave the past in the past."

Delia's no nonsense tone ended Lexie's questioning. "I'll ask Ruben if he'll work part time for the rest of the year."

"He's in his seventies, may not want a day job," Delia warned.

"I'll soon find out," Lexie went out the door.

Ruben and Sam nodded their heads in unison as Lexie approached the bench. "Ruben, I could use an extra deputy."

"How's that?"

"Tye's out of state which has left us short-handed. I also want your expertise related to my father's murder."

"I decided that a drifter killed Nodin. No evidence that a local did it." Ruben ran his fingers through his thinning grey hair.

"I know, Ruben, but he's my father. Surely you understand why I want to reopen his case? Lots of new technology and after all these years, maybe someone's tongue will loosen up."

"I get it."

"You'll work 8 a.m. to 3 p.m., five days a week—nothing heavy duty. Take care of speeding and parking citations. Also, answer the phone during Delia's lunch break. I need a backup man until the first of the year, then we'll have enough city money allotted to hire a full-time deputy."

Ruben's hand formed a cup around his chin, and his fingers massaged his cheeks. He glanced at Sam. "I could use extra money. Social Security doesn't stretch far enough. I'd like to contribute to the case. If we find you're father's killer it'd make up for my past failure." He looked at Sam again.

"I think you should go for it," Sam approved. "A novelty that an old man is wanted for anything. Who knows, maybe I'll find myself a dancing job." Sam boxed Ruben's shoulder and laughed at his own joke.

Ruben saluted Lexie, "I'll give it a try but don't expect me to chase after a felon— unless she's using a walker."

Lexie returned the salute, "It's a deal. Can you start tomorrow?"

"I can. Got a prior appointment today on this bench with my pal."

"Check in at 8 a.m. Delia will have your paperwork ready."

Lexie walked past them into Dixie's restaurant. The red gingham curtains and tablecloths were as cheerful as the proprietor's attitude.

Dixie fingered the order pad. Her stiff red hair looked like a beehive protruding from her head. Dangling fake-emerald earrings and a green satin bow gave the finishing touches to her appearance. Lexie found it unbelievable that this woman was Margo's best friend. Dixie was as cultured as an ape at the opera.

Dixie pulled a pen from behind her ear, "What are you hungry for today?"

"Delia already called in two cheeseburger baskets to go."

"What's that rock on your hand, girl?"

"In December, I'm happy to announce, I'll become Mrs. Red Anderson."

"Damn, that's good news. Your Mom always thought you'd wind up an old maid." Dixie gave her lips a soft slap. "Oops, sorry, don't mean to piss you off."

"Believe me, you're words are no surprise!"

"Your mom coming back for the wedding?"

"Hope so," Lexie took the offered bag and escaped more questions.

Back at the office, she pulled a chair to Delia's desk.

Pen in hand, Delia pushed her burger and fries aside for more important pursuits. "Have you thought about your wedding colors?"

"Not really."

"Gold is pretty. Red poinsettias are easy to decorate with in December. Attendants can wear gold dresses and carry two or three poinsettia stems."

"Sounds lovely. I want it simple. As you know, I'm no girlie-girl."

"Who are your attendants?"

"I thought one was enough, but Red will probably ask Tye and Adam. I'll ask Jamie and Beth. I won't invite my college friends to a wedding mixed with a murder investigation."

Delia's eyes widened, "How's Beth doing?"

"Better than expected considering Bud slung her down basement steps, then set the house on fire. She limps, but I think she'll do this for me."

"She should since you saved her life. Loretta?"

Lexie's face looked like a sharp pain assaulted her body. "No way. I won't listen to her gripe on my wedding day. She always manages to rub in how my mom wanted me to be like her. Nothing but a fake friend."

"You and Red get that wedding list started. We'll travel to the city next Saturday to look at dresses and pick out the invitations." Delia paused, "That's assuming you want my company?"

"You're my favorite lady in the world. Of course you must come."

Delia reached for a tissue.

Chapter Twenty

At 8 p.m. Tye and Adam handed their empty dinner plates to the waitress at the Happy Steer Restaurant.

"Not sure about the name of this place, son. Would a steer be happy slaughtered and thrown on a flame?"

"Probably should call the place Pissed Off Steer," Adam quipped.

Tye fingered his dirty napkin, "This day was a waste of time."

"We learned the business owners know nothing."

"An optimistic point of view, Adam. I guess there's some worth in ruling out things that aren't helpful."

Adam nodded.

Tye dropped a tip on the table. "Let's stop at the burger place, so you can question the teens. About nine o'clock we'll visit the two bars on First Street, then hit the Pier Bar between ten and ten-thirty, probably about the time the fun begins. We'll head home before midnight."

"No luck," Adam reported after his thirty-minute tromp and talk around Burger Station.

Tye breathed a heavy sigh, "Okay, the bars are our last hope."

The bartenders at the first two places offered nothing, nor did the patrons that were still sober. "Last stop," Tye parked the Avalanche beside a building that seemed to float by the shore.

The exterior that was once painted white was now gray wood. The rusty hinges let out a loud squeal as Tye pulled the door open and allowed Adam first entrance.

A beer bottle flew across the room and smashed against the wall a foot from them. Glass fragments bombarded the pair. Specks of blood burst out on the right side of Adam's face. The bartender's gravelly voice ground into Adam's head. "What the hell are you doin' here you little shit? I told you to stay out of my place or I'd tear off your balls and stuff them down your throat. You think you can screw my wife, and I'll serve you a drink?"

The man was around five-feet-eight inches and a wall of solid muscle. A vertical tattoo that said *Boss* decorated the bartender's upper arm.

The bully rounded the bar and jabbed his pointer finger repeatedly against the middle of Adam's chest. He didn't say a single word in defense.

Tye grabbed the stubby finger, "Hold it, man!"

"Damn if I'll hold anything, you asshole." The bartender struggled to release his finger from Tye's vise.

"This is my boy, Adam. He's from Oklahoma."

"You lyin' bastard. You think my eyes can't see Snake right in front of me? I'm nobody's fool."

"You're mistaken."

Boss's thick hand went to Adam's throat.

Tye circled Boss and put an elbow lock around his neck.

"Let him go, man. He's not Snake." With every word Tye squeezed Boss's neck a little tighter.

Adam gagged and choked from Boss's ever tightening grip. He started a downward spiral to the floor. Tye released the bully to catch his son's fall.

A foot swung forward and slammed into Adam's ribs. Tye fell on top of him and took the brunt of the kicks. Grabbing a pointy cowboy boot with one hand, he shoved the attacker back. Next, a dirty work boot came toward his head. He gripped the boot and twisted. The aggressor fell backwards.

The bar filled with angry bellows. "Get that Injun! Smash his head!"

Those were the last words Tye heard before the world went black. The pair ended up in a pile of unconscious flesh.

"Take them out of here," Boss ordered.

The man with the pointy boots ripped Adam's shirt, exposing his left shoulder. "This ain't Snake. No snake head on his shoulder."

"You're shittin' me." Boss took a drag from a liquor bottle, "It's Snake's face."

"It ain't him," the man chided.

Boss hollered across the room, "Duke and Slinger, I'll give you a hundred to throw away the pair."

The grimy men fisted the offered money, then drug the bodies out the side door. They laid Tye across the second row seat and stuffed Adam into a sitting position on the passenger side. Duke drove the Avalanche while Slinger followed on his Harley.

Miles later they reached the scenic drop off at Nevel Falls. Duke slowly drove the truck forward. A couple of feet from the edge, he released the brake and jumped out. He and Slinger pushed the vehicle. The Chevy hovered in the air a few seconds, then plowed downward toward the ravine that housed the river.

Duke straddled behind Slinger as he drove the cycle back to the bar for a few well-deserved rounds.

Chapter Twenty-One

Lexie was eager to discuss Nodin's murder with Rubin. As she drove, an underlying current of dread periodically poked its unwanted presence into her chest.

She tried to determine the cause of her foreboding. Actually, her life was at a peak: an upcoming marriage and a murder case that she'll solve or resolve by year's end. If no new information comes from the investigation, she'll face the fact that there's no definitive answer. She isn't so obsessed that she'll continue the futile task of searching for a killer who left no clues.

When Lexie arrived, Delia was leaning over the white conference table pointing to spaces that Ruben neglected to fill.

"Mornin' boss," Ruben said.

Delia grinned, "Yep, morning boss."

"You two started the paper trail."

"Can't see this small print, even with my bifocals," Ruben complained.

"True," Delia agreed, "but I'm here to assist."

"And fine help you are," he praised.

Lexie made a few calls while they completed the paperwork.

Ruben stretched, "What next?"

"Stay where you are and we'll work at the table." Lexie recovered a twelve-by-twelve cardboard box from the bottom file drawer and set it on the table. The name N. Wolfe was printed on both ends and the top.

Ruben eyed the box, "That looks familiar. Time sure wears on things. Top smashed in and all the corners mangled."

"That wear indicates that you spent hours with the contents." Lexie pulled the lid off to reveal a collection of items. She'd spent hours scrutinizing them. Her hope continued that she'd find a clue that validated continued work on the case.

"Yep, I had it memorized. Your dad was a good man, deserved better than he got out of life."

"Let's talk about the people you interviewed, and if there was a particular reason why." Lexie pulled Ruben's old notes from the box. "Says you interviewed all the closest neighbors."

"I did, but worthless considering no one lived within five miles of your folk's place. Prather family and Willie Anderson lived the closest."

"I forgot that Larry Prather lived that close. Who is Willie Anderson?"

"He's the brother of Red's father, Kurt."

"Never heard of him."

"He was my primary suspect; a low life. Kurt took him in 'cause he was family. Had robbery convictions out of state. Lazy bum lived off Kurt and Lora for a few months, then they moved to Springdale, Arkansas. Willie soon left for parts unknown since there was no one to buy or cook his meals."

Lexie's back straightened, "Any proof he did it?"

"He was a suspect because of his criminal history. Also, Larry claimed he saw Willie drive down the road that day, but that means nothing." Ruben pulled a yellowed paper from the box. "This is what your mom identified as stolen."

Lexie reread the familiar list. Nodin's wallet was emptied and thrown on the floor. Half dozen pieces of Mom's jewelry: cubic zirconia broach, a pair of diamond earrings, fake pearl necklace, gold earrings, silver watch, and an opal ring with a large stone set in the middle surrounded by six smaller ones.

Ruben's features tightened, "Not much to kill a man over."

"Paper says you interviewed Judge Simpson, Attorney Cecil Lansbury, and Mayor Clayton."

Ruben took a sudden interest in the water dispenser.

"What's the connection between my father's murder and these esteemed Diffee citizens?"

Ruben gulped water, then choked momentarily. His eyes met Delia's for a fleeting second.

"Join us at the table, Delia," Lexie's tone was peppered with irritation. "You two work for me. What aren't you telling me?"

Delia's lips clamped. Her eyes examined the tabletop.

Lexie's voice pierced the air, "Cough it up, Ruben."

"Remember you asked for it."

"Go ahead," Lexie directed.

"Your mother was the common factor. At some point in their lives, all of these men were . . . not sure of the correct word."

"Obsessed," was Delia's soft contribution.

Ruben nodded, "Obsessed fits. Margo wrapped men around her little finger, then flicked them off like a booger when she finished with them. She dissected more hearts than a cardiologist."

Lexie's words came out slow, "You thought my father was murdered because the killer loved my mother?"

"It was considered. My final theory, however, was a drifter robbed and murdered Nodin."

Lexie confronted Delia, "Did Margo break up your relationship with Cecil?"

Delia grunted "yes" through clinched teeth.

"And you didn't take him back, which meant Margo screwed up his life. Since he lost his love, perhaps he didn't want Margo to have her love either. Did he ever threaten Margo or Nodin?"

Delia defended, "I never heard him threaten anyone. Cecil is a good man. Anyway, we were together in our twenties. That was years before your dad was murdered."

"What about the judge and mayor?"

Ruben rubbed his temples. "Well, the judge's wife had a muscle disease. She was in bad shape. No one had the heart to tell her about her wayward husband. The mayor's wife divorced him and left town. That was about five years before your father died."

Lexie blubbered, "Did my mother have sex with all these men?"

Delia's countenance changed, "She was a temptress, not a whore. She was beautiful, resembled Elizabeth Taylor. She played with men, like a cat cornering a mouse. As soon as she took Cecil away from me, she dumped him. I know this is unkind to say about your mother, Lexie, but she was a terrible person."

A vague feeling indicated that Lexie should defend her mother, but a stronger emotion dwarfed that one. "One of Margo's 'mice' may have killed my father to get revenge. Perhaps someone wanted her heart broken, just as his was.

"Possible," Ruben agreed.

Lexie read from notes, "This is our list for now: Cecil, Judge Simpson, Willie Anderson, and Clayton."

"Telling your fiancé that his uncle is a murder suspect will cause a war of words," Ruben predicted.

"Probably not as difficult as telling Clay his dad is one," Lexie replied.

"Clayton will raise hell when he's identified as a suspect," Delia added as she limped toward the ringing phone.

Delia whispered, "It's Jamie—she's crying."

"Jamie, it's Lexie."

"They didn't come home," Jamie sobbed out the words. "I talked to Tye at ten o'clock. He said they were stopping at one more bar. They were supposed to return early this morning. Lexie, it's almost noon. I've tried to phone them a hundred times. The newspaper said that Adam didn't show for work. Something has happened to them. I know it."

Lexie heard Jamie suck in the air that she hadn't remembered to breathe. Lexie almost assured her that everything was okay, no point in getting upset, but she stopped herself. She remembered another phone call a few months ago. Abbey phoned, afraid someone was murdering players from her old high school basketball team. Lexie told Abbey her fears didn't warrant an investigation. Twenty-four hours later, Abbey was dead.

"I'll give Sloan the heads up, then take off for Kansas."

"Pick me up on the way out of town," Jamie instructed.

"No point in you coming."

"The point is these are the two people I love most in the world. I can't just sit here. I either go with you or by myself." Jamie's words seemed more like hysteria than an ultimatum.

"Okay, pack a bag. I'll go home for a few things, then come get you. Bring something sexy to wear."

Lexie quickly punched in Sloan's number. "Sheriff Sloan, it's Lexie. Have you seen my brother?"

"Not since yesterday morning."

"He and Adam never made it home. I'm on my way there."

"I'll start tracking them down," Sloan stated.

"Thanks."

Delia grimaced and blinked hard, but her tears overflowed anyway.

"Ruben, please stay until Clay gets here at 6 p.m."

"Sure, no problem."

"I'll phone as soon as we find them," Lexie promised.

Chapter Twenty-Two

When Lexie's Jeep screeched to a stop, Jamie ran down her front porch steps. She stooped as she got into the vehicle, then folded her nearly six-foot frame onto the front seat. Her fists turned white as she clutched a small bag against her belly.

Lexie glanced at Jamie. Her hair was pulled back. Red blotches spotted her face and neck. Anxiety and fear had taken its toll.

"Sloan called back, no news on the guys. He was told that two men were asking questions around town, which he already knew. He questioned three bartenders. The first two acknowledged Tye and Adam were there. The third guy reported that no strangers asked questions around his place. He added that out-of-towners didn't come near his bar because they feared the motorcycle gangs."

"They disappeared between 10:00 and 10:30 p.m." Jamie pressed her lips together, but the groan escaped anyway.

"We'll find them, Jamie."

Finally out of town, the highway stretched in front of them for endless miles. This was the first time Lexie had evidenced vulnerability in Jamie. The woman was a college women's basketball coach, and generally tough as nails. Even though Tye and Jamie were a couple off and on since high school, the two women kept their distance.

The fire changed that. Nothing like two women trapped in a flaming basement to start the bonding process. Jamie refused to leave the injured Beth and helped Lexie get her to safety. They pushed Loretta out the window first to get her to shut up. She screamed that she was dying, that it was too late for Beth. They probably should've left Loretta in the flames. Instead they saved her—questionable logic, but the right thing to do. "I was thinking about our time in the flames. Why was it we saved Loretta?"

Jamie's laugh was genuine, "I think the smoke clogged our brains."

"My theory is that we pushed her out the window so we couldn't hear her screams."

"That conclusion works for me," Jamie agreed. "Loretta has been busy the last few months getting her house rebuilt and buying new furniture."

"Do you think her near death-experience made her a better person?"

Jamie shook her head, "A resounding 'no' to that. Now she thinks she's some sort of super hero who reappeared out of the ashes. Apparently, we're lucky she's still here to tell everybody what to do."

"I knew I was dreaming. She is who she is."

"Your ring is beautiful."

Lexie held her hand in model mode. "Thank you and I agree. Will you be my maid-of-honor?"

Jamie did a double take, obviously a little surprised by the invitation. "Of course, I'm thrilled. Who else are you asking?"

"Beth, but I haven't yet."

"She'll be excited. She'd do anything for her heroine."

The interior of the car went silent. Lexie reasoned that staying off the main subject only works for a while, then grim reality returns.

"Did you remember to bring your slut outfit?"

Jamie's eyes widened, "I did, but I'm curious as to why I require prostitute apparel?"

"We both know Tye wouldn't skip that last bar, so that's our starting point. We'll change our clothes at the motel, then find new friends."

The motel sign flashed a welcome of sorts. They missed supper, but neither was interested in food. They changed clothes and put on make-up in preparation for their bar visit. The time was near 11 p.m., so the place should be in full swing.

Chapter Twenty-Three

Lexie worried that her tight black skirt might hike and reveal the tiny derringer strapped around her inner thigh. Her midriff was bare below the short, scoop-necked purple top that revealed cleavage with each downward movement.

Jamie's black hot pants hugged her butt. Her breasts were clearly defined beneath an orange knit tee.

They shared a tube of red lipstick. Neither of them wore much make-up, so getting heavy eyeliner on straight was a trick. Mascara perked up their eyelashes. They stood beside each other in front of the mirror. Lexie felt like a midget beside Jamie, but her gun made a good equalizer.

Jamie smiled for the second time that day, "Well, sister, we are two hot sleazebags."

Lexie got directions to the bar from the motel clerk. She also got an offer she was glad to refuse.

The highway veered off to a graveled road that snaked toward a large shack on the riverbank. No lights lit the darkness that surrounded the bar. A half dozen motorcycles and four trucks occupied the dirt parking lot.

"Stay here, Jamie. Lock the door. I'll check out the area."

The heels she wore hampered furtive movement. She rounded the end of the building. A patio of sorts stuck out from the building's side. A picket fence surrounded the area that held old picnic tables with deteriorating benches. A door led from the deck into the bar.

The man, who glanced at her as she peeked in the bathroom window, didn't seem the least bit disturbed. *Maybe he'll think his liquored state brought on delusions.*

She retrieved a penlight from her purse and examined the deck. Periodic blood smears led from the exit down the steps. Her worst fear was coming true. No, the bodies thrown in the river was the worst outcome. Someone dragged the body or bodies down the steps, then picked them up and carried them. The water was too shallow around the bar to conceal a body. The flow stopped at the inlet so the water couldn't carry a body down the river, she hoped.

Lexie scraped a spot of blood and placed it in the ever-present plastic bag in her purse. Her steps were purposeful as she approached the Jeep window, but the ache in her chest left her weak.

She tapped on the window, "It's show time."

Jamie's voice prickled with underlying fear, "Did you find anything?"

Lexie scanned the bar's entrance, "No sign of them or the Avalanche."

The women entered a double door that looked like it was repossessed from a barn. The chaotic intensity of multiple conversations switched to wolf whistles.

"Come here, my pretties," Boss summoned. "I'll start you two off with free drinks for giving me something to look at besides all these ugly male mugs."

Jamie forced a smile, "You're making my dream come true."

Boss focused on the outline of her breasts under the thin knit shirt. "Ah sweetheart, you got the equipment to make all my dreams come true."

A skinny man with a scraggly beard and stained clothes pressed up against Lexie. "I like what you got baby. Oops, I dropped my napkin. Why don't you pick it up for me?"

"I know what you're up to mister, trying to get a look at my girls." Lexie gave his upper arm a soft squeeze.

"See, Slinger, she's smart and pretty," the pointy-boot man said. "You gals here for a drink, a lay, or something else?"

Lexie recited her lie, "I'm here 'cause my old man said he wanted a beer and never came home. I figure he spent the night with his wife and left me cold. He's a big Indian fellow. Did you see him?"

Slinger's laugh burst out with a spray of spit, "Don't worry, I'm sure he got his due."

Boss's glare pierced into Slinger's face. "Ain't seen no one around here that fits your description!" The angry scowl didn't awaken Slinger to the fact that Boss was on the verge of strangling him.

Lexie squeezed Slinger's shoulder, "If you were the one who gave him his due, you've earned a good time."

"Sweetheart, I gave it to him, and I'm ready for my reward." He poked his face into her neck, slobbering smelly spit onto her skin.

"Hold up, man," Jamie intervened. "Your friends all got nosey eyes. Come outside with us and we'll double your pleasure."

"Take the whores and go," Boss ordered. "Keep your filthy mouth shut."

Each woman grabbed an arm and escorted Slinger out. He dropped his pants outside the open Jeep door, "Who's first?"

Lexie pressed the barrel of her derringer in his temple. "I want the Indian man. You'll tell me what happened to him, or you'll soon have a hole in your head."

"You crazy bitches better let me go." He spit toward Lexie's face, pushed Jamie, then ran with his pants slipping downward.

Lexie aimed and hit her target—his butt.

"Oh no, oh no, I'm shot," he screeched as he attempted to run forward. His pants gathered around his knees and propelled him face down into dirt and gravel.

No movement disturbed the bar door, everyone inside oblivious to the parking lot drama.

Lexie stood over him, the gun aimed at his chest, "Stand up!"

"I can't. I got a bullet in my butt, remember?"

"You'll have one in your right arm, left arm, right leg, left leg, and your head if you don't start talking."

Slinger stood and limped toward her. "I didn't want to do it. Boss made us. If we didn't obey, he'd have hurt us bad."

"I'm getting mighty pissed, Slinger. I won't hurt you. I'll kill you. What happened to the two men who came in the bar?"

He stammered, "My butt is bleeding. Get me a doctor."

"No doctor until I know what happened to the strangers."

"No way, I'd be beat raw if I told you whores anything."

Lexie walked a few yards, then turned and fired a shot at his right arm.

Blood spread on his dirty tee shirt, "Shit, shit, you're psycho."

"I'm crazy and I'll fill you with holes until you talk. The good news is you'll bleed to death before I put a bullet in your head."

Slinger slumped, "I'm feelin' faint."

Jamie waved her cell phone in the air, "Talk fast and I'll phone an ambulance."

Lexie aimed her gun at his left arm, and words spilled from Slinger's mouth.

"Duke and I crammed them into the truck. Duke drove the truck and I followed on my Harley to the Ravine, three miles east. Duke pushed the truck over the cliff and we hightailed it out of there. If you repeat my story, I'll say you're lyin' whores."

"Call 911, Jamie. Report a gunshot victim in the parking lot then hang up."

Chapter Twenty-Four

Lexie and Jamie stared into the dark abyss called the Ravine. The grass was flattened near the edge, making the possibility even stronger that a vehicle flew over the side.

Lexie dug her phone out, "Sloan, it's Lexie. I'm at the top of the Ravine. I received a report that Tye's truck went off the edge."

"I'll notify all emergency services, then get right there."

The women cautiously walked downward for a few yards. Only the small beam from a penlight and a full moon lit the way.

"It's been over twenty-four hours. Is it possible that they're alive?" Jamie's words conveyed restrained terror.

"Tye's probably is working on excuses for missing work." Lexie tried to cover her fear with a cheerful tone, but it only garbled her words.

A siren wailed in the distance. Lexie assumed it was for Slinger. A few minutes later, a line of patrol cars, fire trucks, and ambulances snaked up the incline.

Searchlights lit the night sky. Rescuers focused the LED white light down the hill. Men in heavy boots and headgear moved toward the ledge then disappeared.

After a couple of hours, the echoes of pounding and chainsaws drifted upward from the dark dungeon below. The jaws-of-life arrived during the second hour and was eased downward. The noise from below stopped abruptly. Jamie and Lexie sat on a giant rock. Labored breathing and sniffles escaped their bodies.

After three more hours they heard boots tromp toward them. The women ran toward the rescuers. Three men on each side toted a cot with a motionless body on its surface. The men paused for a moment as Jamie bent to kiss Tye. Lexie squeezed his hand.

"Glad you dropped by," he joked. Blood dripped onto his mangled artificial leg. Lines of dried blood on his face traced to a gash on his head. "Adam?"

"They're bringing him up," Lexie assured. "Jamie, ride in the ambulance with Tye and I'll stay with Adam." She waited for her nephew as the siren's roar diminished to silence.

Adam's dark eyes widened at the sight of Lexie. Glass fragments were embedded in the side of his face, and his neck was bruised. A medic indicated that Adam's leg was broken.

"Nephew, you have quite the story to write."

"No kidding," was his subdued reply. "How'd you find us?"

"Used sweet talk and a few bullets."

"Dad okay?"

"Looked as ornery as ever."

Adam's voice trembled, "If it weren't for a large boulder, we'd have died in the ravine."

Lexie held his hand, "But you didn't die and you'll both recover. I'll follow the ambulance."

The men lifted Adam into the emergency vehicle.

Chapter Twenty-Five

Lexie leaned back in the recliner beside Tye's hospital bed. He consumed his breakfast like a starving critter, barely swallowed one bite before cramming the next one into his mouth. Jamie was downstairs with Adam for x-rays. Sloan, seated in a chair near the foot of the bed, was eager to hear Tye's story.

Tye told them about the bar fight and truck crash. His lips formed into a sad smirk when he joked about having a son called Snake.

"Apparently, my lost son is a hell raiser. Boss attacked Adam because he thought Adam was Snake. That's what started the fight. Once a bottle hit my head, I didn't become conscious again until after the truck smashed against a boulder. I heard Adam ask if I was okay. No way we could get out, and we tried plenty."

"Lucky your sister found you," Sloan remarked with a suspicious sneer toward Lexie.

"I figured she would. It pisses her off when I don't show-up at work."

"Funny coincidence, Tye. That guy you mentioned was found in the bar parking lot with a bullet in his ass and another in his arm." Sloan's eyes studied Lexie's face while he spoke.

"Not surprised," Tye offered. "He and his buddies were a mean loco crew."

"Slinger said a crazy whore shot him. By the way, Lexie, do you have a gun with you?"

"Sure, my Sig 220."

"Slinger was shot with a little derringer."

Lexie met his judgmental stare, "I used to carry one, but got rid of it. Not intimidating enough."

"Hmm," was Sloan's final comment on Slinger's whore. "I've got a sting planned at the bar tonight. I'll bring them all in and close the place down. You'll need to identify these guys, Tye, when I get them locked up."

"It would be my pleasure," Tye saluted.

Sloan tipped his hat to Lexie and quasi marched from the room.

A soon as the door closed behind Sloan, a burst of laughter erupted from Tye's mouth. "Damn, Lexie, you're one badass. A shot in the rear?"

"His fault. He didn't tell me what I wanted to know."

"I'm not messing with you anymore, Sis. If you say it, I'll do it. I don't want a doctor digging bullets out of my butt."

"Finally, you've come to your senses."

Adam was wheeled in as the last fragment of laughter disappeared.

"You're a happy duo," Jamie remarked.

"Discussing my badass sister."

"You're very fortunate to have such a sister." Jamie planted a kiss on his cheek.

"I know, I know. Let's not get all mushy." Tye squinted, "Thanks, Badass."

"Anytime."

"What about the x-rays, son?"

"Leg is broken—won't cast for a day or so because of the swelling."

Lexie stood, "I must return to Diffee. I left Clay, Ruben, and Delia to fend for themselves. I'll return in three or four days to drive you home."

"Mom's on her way here," Jamie informed. She'll drive us home."

"I promise I'll help with Dad's case as soon as I get home. I'm sorry I haven't been around."

"I'll hold you to it." Lexie gave the men each a kiss on their foreheads and returned Jamie's vivacious hug. She hurried out the door, hoping no one saw the tears she smoothed into her cheeks.

Chapter Twenty-Six

Delia reported by phone that everything went 'smooth as silk,' so Lexie didn't stop at the office. Her unreleased fears pounded in her head. After two pain pills, the cymbals in her head stopped banging, and she collapsed onto the soft mattress.

The newspaper hitting her front door woke her from a sound sleep the next morning. She looked out the window before snatching the newspaper off the front step in her tee shirt and panties.

She flopped on the sofa, her eyes focused on the headline—SHERIFF WOLFE SAVES TWO LOCALS. That was their boy Adam. Somehow he called in the story in spite of a broken leg and multiple injuries. He told the tale so vividly, she felt his pain and fear.

During the drive to her office, she made a mental list of what needed accomplished. All the drama around Naomi's murder and Tye's son removed her focus from her dad's murder. Hopefully, all the extraneous problems would stop long enough so that she could jail a killer and marry Red in December.

Delia and Ruben occupied their designated chairs when she arrived. Delia met her with a hug.

Ruben shook his head, "You're really something, girl!"

Lexie smiled, "My nephew is a bit biased."

Delia sat, "I doubt it."

Lexie retrieved the box and set it on the table. "Okay, Ruben, let's give it another try."

Rubin rubbed his chin, "Something didn't seem right. Couldn't figure it out at first, but then it hit me last night. The murder weapon wasn't in the box."

Lexie gasped, "You mean it was in the box before?"

"Yep, everything was in that box; the knife in a plastic bag."

"I pulled the box from the courthouse basement and brought it here. There was no knife and it wasn't listed," Lexie recounted, "I assumed it was never found."

"It was a Kodiak hunting knife, had a fancy decorative handle with a hundred or so grooves. Kind of antique looking," Ruben explained.

Lexie's words flooded out, "With the current DNA technology, a lab can check if there's DNA embedded in the recesses of the handle. We've got to find that knife, Ruben."

"Damn if we don't."

"Interesting that the murder weapon disappeared from the location where three of our prime suspects have easy access: a lawyer, a judge, and a mayor."

Lexie's words fueled Delia's anger, "I told you, Cecil is a good man. He doesn't hurt people."

Ruben nodded, "Probably not him. In my original investigation, he looked clean. If I recall correctly, he was out of town."

Lexie eyes darkened, "I didn't find case notes that indicated Cecil was out of town."

Ruben's finger tapped his forehead, "Stored up here!"

Lexie felt venom rush through her veins. She wondered what else he didn't bother to write down that might solve her father's case. *What kind of sheriff doesn't log in the murder weapon?"*

"Back in the old days, we didn't have fancy computers to do our work," Ruben defended.

She controlled her tongue. "Cecil was around forty-seven when Dad died. According to what you said the other day, Delia, you were both in your mid-twenties when Margo ruined your relationship. I can't imagine that Cecil waited years to pay back my mother."

"Unless?"

"Unless what, Ruben?"

He looked cautiously at Delia. "Unless something happened that brought the pain back."

Lexie confronted, "What happened, Delia?"

Delia glared at Ruben, "Ask Cecil, I didn't track his comings and goings."

Chapter Twenty-Seven

Saturday morning brought a call from Tye that they were home and doing well.

The dishes were washed, the bathroom scrubbed, and the floors mopped. Lexie hadn't cleaned this much in weeks. She knew what motivated her now—avoidance of a conversation with her mother.

After the laundry was finished, she pushed in the numbers. "It's me, Mom." Chilled silence met her greeting.

"Sure took long enough for you to call. Dixie told me a week ago about your engagement, and Loretta called the day after."

"Why did Loretta call?"

"Asked me to stay with her, said your place was small and gloomy. Her house is remodeled with new furniture. She was excited for me to see it! Too bad you didn't inherit my decorating talent."

"We'll spend the night of the rehearsal at the house Red remodeled. The other nights are up to you."

"I'm so busy—not sure I can make it!"

"I'm sure you can find a way for your only daughter. Did Dixie or Loretta tell you that you have a grandson living in Diffee?"

"I almost passed out when I heard the boy is almost twenty."

"Mom, you're fifty-nine, old enough to be a granny."

"Don't be cruel, Lexie. That word sounds ancient. He'll have to call me something else."

A smile teased at Lexie's lips, "I'm sure Adam will call you something else once he gets to know you."

"Did you ever have a plastic surgeon look at that scar on your face?"

"I'm used to it."

"Well, I'm not! Makes me sad. You were such a pretty little girl. Actually, I won't come if I feel bad every time I look at you."

"Why do you feel bad, Mother? Do you blame yourself?"

"Lose that attitude if you want me at your wedding."

"Sorry, please come. You're my hostess. You know I have no talent for that stuff."

"I know you don't. I'll rearrange my schedule this once."

"Got to hang up, Mom. I'm meeting Jamie, Beth, and Delia. We're going to Fayetteville to select my dress and the bridesmaid dresses."

"You should invite Loretta. At least she has some taste. Dixie said that Delia is big as a barn."

Lexie lashed out, "Delia's beautiful inside and out."

Margo accentuated her words, "Gosh, I didn't mean anything bad—just talking."

"Phone when your plane reservations are made. I'll pick you up at the airport."

"No, thanks. I'll rent a car and arrive in style. Call me when you know your colors, so I can have my dress made. Bye."

"Okay."

Lexie massaged her forehead. She had no desire to phone her mother back about colors or anything else.

Chapter Twenty-Eight

Tye talked to Seth and Gabriel when he was in Kansas, but today was his first chance to see them.

Myrna walked out Paula's front door as Tye opened the gate. "How are they doing?"

"Oh, pretty well. They're both in play therapy. Seth talks more and Gabriel cries less, that's progress. Seth has the ball by the front door waiting for your return," Myrna smiled.

"They're great little guys. I hope you find them a good family. Seth said that he'd never had a daddy."

"That's true from what I've learned. Both boys were the result of one-night stands. We put the adoption announcement in the newspaper, but no response so far."

"Will someone in Naomi's family adopt them?"

Myrna shook her head, "No, thank God. Her mom is a huffer who looks like she's on death's door. Naomi's sister died as a result of smelling spray paint."

"I'm sorry to hear that."

"Psychologist recommended that the boys be placed with someone they know—that left Paula . . . and you."

"Paula's a good choice."

"She doesn't have the patience or desire to raise two, spirited little boys."

"Will the system let a single man adopt the boys?"

"A man, like you, who has a relationship with the kids, the answer is yes." Her eyes brightened, "Do you think it's a possibility?"

"Never thought about it."

"Please consider it. The sooner they have a permanent home the better. If you decide to take the leap, come by the office Monday, and we'll start the paperwork." With her words left hanging in the air, Myrna walked to her Honda.

Tye sat down on the step. *She's insane. I can't handle fatherhood!*

The screen door banged behind him, then small arms wrapped around his neck. "Someone got me," Tye bellowed, "Oh no! Who is it?" Gabriel's giggles tickled his ear as he pulled the boy to his lap.

Seth stood patiently at the edge of the porch with a ball in his hand. "Do you want to play catch?"

"Can't do it, my throwing arm is only activated by a Seth hug." Seth pushed his body against Tye's side. He pulled him close. One small Seth kiss made contact with his temple.

Chapter Twenty-Nine

"Thanks, Ruben, I appreciate you working on Saturday," Lexie walked toward his desk.

"No problem. I see Sam kept the bench warm for me. I'll hightail it across the street. See you Monday."

Ruben gave Tye a high five on his way out.

"Where were you, Bro?" Lexie questioned.

"I visited the boys."

"How are they?"

"Better," Tye slowly exhaled, "If I adopted the guys, would you have me institutionalized?"

Lexie couldn't keep a straight face. "Many times I've considered your actions emotionally unstable, but not this time."

"Very funny!" Tye argued with himself, "No, I won't adopt them. I can't handle all the baggage that comes with parenting."

"I'd help and I'm sure Delia and Jamie would also. The boys already know Paula. They'd have a familiar daycare."

His words stormed out, "Are you trying to talk me into this craziness?"

Lexie's hands rose, "Cool down, Bro, I volunteered to assist, that's all."

"Hell, I can't adopt them. Don't know how to care for anyone but myself." Tye directed his comment toward the papers on his desk.

The door flew open and Delia rushed in, "Consider yourself warned, Loretta is with Beth."

Sinking dread formed in the pit of Lexie's stomach, "Oh no, how can that be? Shoot me! Just shoot me!"

"Surprise," Loretta called, "I'm here to save the day."

Lexie cringed, "Wow, this is a surprise."

Beth stood behind Loretta mouthing "not me" and shaking her head no.

"Your mom invited me, said you ladies required style advice."

Tye's hand covered his smile.

Lexie was speechless, which didn't matter since Loretta carried the conversation by herself.

"Let's eat at that wonderful restaurant on Second Street," Loretta didn't wait for a response.

Delia peered out the window, "Jamie's arrived. Let's get moving."

"We'll take my BMW," Loretta insisted.

Lexie shook her head when Jamie's eyes bugged at the sight of Loretta. "Mom invited Loretta because she's classy, unlike the rest of us."

"Hmm," Jamie responded.

"Come on, long legs, you sit in the front," Loretta directed Jamie, "Let those short girls get in the back."

Jamie bowed, "Yes, your high-ass."

Loretta missed the joke; too busy primping in the rearview mirror.

Lexie wished she was shooting bad guys, bullets flying. That sounded like a tranquil day compared to this one.

Chapter Thirty

Lexie studied the crack in the ceiling Monday morning as she lay in bed. There was a chance the previous Saturday was one of the ten worst days of her life. The day was consumed with Delia's hurt feelings, Jamie's biting comments to Loretta, and Loretta's never-ending flow of advice. It was soft-spoken Beth who finally shut her up. Beth took her aside and whispered, "You keep forgetting it's Lexie's wedding."

Loretta pouted for the rest of the shopping trip, which was a welcome relief from her flapping tongue.

Lexie crawled from bed and retrieved the white satin gown. She brushed out her hair and slid the dress over her body. The slim style accentuated her curves, and the rounded neckline, decorated with tiny pearls, revealed a little cleavage. The satin-lined lace train was eight feet long. It also was embellished with tiny pearls.

Loretta tried verbal force to get her into a wide skirted, triple ruffled dress with a strapless top. A beautiful dress, but too frilly for Lexie. When Jamie,

Beth and Delia cheered Lexie's choice, Loretta got angry, again.

They didn't find any gold bridesmaid dresses. They bought royal blue velvet dresses instead. Loretta's final blow came when Lexie told her there were two bridesmaids. That information kept her quiet for a full five minutes before she discussed flower arrangements that Lexie couldn't afford.

"Sorry, Loretta, the flowers are already planned," Lexie informed her gently.

"I'll tell your mother I tried and failed," Loretta's final words as she let them out at the sheriff's office.

Lexie turned in front of the mirror. In spite of it all, the day was a success because she found a gorgeous wedding gown.

Lexie traded the gown for her uniform, twisted her braid into a knot, and sped out the door. She wanted to catch Cecil Lansbury before he headed to the courthouse.

When she arrived, his door was ajar, and no secretary sat in the outside lobby. She stood at his office door, "Knock, knock."

"Lexie, come in." He stood, a welcoming smile on his chubby face. "Why do I have the honor of your presence, Sheriff?"

"A couple of things. First, I'm curious about Wanda's case."

"Ah, she pleaded guilty, which made the entire court system happy."

"She didn't have a leg to stand on with all the DNA evidence. I'm relieved Seth didn't have to make a statement," Lexie said.

"I made sure she never found out he actually saw her kill Naomi," Cecil pondered the injustice, "Never know if someone that crazy will go after a child."

"That's true," Lexie responded.

"What was the second thing, Lexie?"

"I reopened my father's murder case, which makes you a suspect—again."

His bushy eyebrows furrowed, "I had no reason to kill Nodin."

"What about getting back at Margo because she ruined your relationship with Delia?"

"If I was going to kill anyone, the logical choice was your shrew of a mother."

Lexie confronted, "The murder weapon disappeared from the evidence box. What happened to it?"

"No idea. If you have any more questions, we'll talk later. I've a court appearance at 8:30 a.m."

"Yes, we'll have more conversations." She offered no words of farewell.

Tye turned as she walked in the door, "Where you been, Sis?"

"I talked to Cecil about Wanda's case. She avoided a lethal injection by pleading guilty."

Delia offered a somber, "Good morning."

Lexie decided not to share all the conversation with Cecil.

"I'm headed to the McAlester prison to interview Wilbur Langley. Based on Ruben's notes, Wilbur was a person of interest in Dad's murder."

"A long shot," Ruben confirmed, "but he was such a low life, he looked suspicious."

"I'll return before Ruben takes off at three."

Lexie was grateful for the calm, patrol car interior. She liked to plan while driving. On this day, however, only scattered thoughts bounced around in her head.

Chapter Thirty-One

"Delia, I'm taking an early lunch. I'll relieve you and Ruben at noon." Tye's rapid steps propelled him out the door and down the sidewalk to the Department of Human Services building. He approached the front desk, "Is Myrna Easton here?"

"I'll see if she's available," the clerk answered.

It wasn't two minutes before Myrna beckoned him to follow down a long hall to the end office.

Tye sat in an old vinyl chair that squealed under his weight. "Your furniture is the same caliber as the sheriff's office."

"Top of the line for all us gov-ment employees," she joked.

"Tell me how this adoption thing works. I probably won't adopt, but I'd like the facts. Does Wilbur have any right to the boys?"

"None. He and Naomi were never married. Regardless of that, he doesn't have rights as a stepfather."

"How about Naomi's mother?"

"Her words, 'Sure as shit don't want any more brats to raise.' Considering her history of prostitution and drug abuse, it's doubtful the court would approve her."

"How about their biological fathers?"

"The state terminates rights in three months when a child has never had a relationship with his father. I filed the paperwork two months ago. The Daily Oklahoman published the Termination of Rights announcement. Eighty days from that publication, if the fathers haven't come forward and made themselves known to the court, their rights are terminated."

Tye swiped the sweat from his forehead, "Do they let a single man adopt?"

"Yes. If you adopt then get married, there's a year wait before your wife can adopt the boys. A private attorney, not DHS, handles that adoption," Myrna explained.

"What are the initial steps?" He backtracked, if I go for it."

"There's a parenting course for people considering adoption, and tons of paperwork. I have a packet right here with Seth and Gabriel written on it."

"Quite a coincidence! Did you see me coming up the walk?"

"No, I saw the way you looked at them the other day."

Tye picked up the packet, "Don't mention this to anyone. I can't say I'll back out 'cause I'm still backing in. I don't want them hurt."

Myrna's voice softened, "I won't say a word, but I will hope and pray."

"I can't stop you from doing that."

"Next adoption class is at 6 p.m. two weeks from today. I hope to see you there."

Tye held the folder against his chest on the way out. Maybe osmosis to his heart would answer his question. Only one thought filled his mind: *What the hell am I doing?*

Chapter Thirty-Two

Lexie pulled into the prison parking lot. Big Mac was its nickname, the place where many of Oklahoma's criminals resided. She wasn't surprised that Wilbur ended up in McAlester, a maximum-security prison. She'd arrested him for making and selling methamphetamines and child endangerment. A look at his criminal record, however, revealed that his younger days were marked by violent behavior. She checked in with the warden who accompanied her to the interrogation room.

Wilbur's gray outfit blended with his ashen complexion. He greeted her with a shallow smile. "I'm torn, Sheriff Girlie. You put me in here, but you saved my life before you did. Not sure whether to like you or spite you."

"Either is okay, Wilbur. I guess you heard that Naomi was murdered by Toby's woman?"

"Yep, I heard it from some of Wanda's kin. That family is mighty proud of their lunatics. That why you're here, Sheriff?"

"I'm here because I heard you have information related to my father's murder." Lexie heard his leg irons rattle under the table as he slammed his feet.

"That's a damn lie. Ruben came after me cause he didn't like me. Wanted a scapegoat."

"So where were you that day, Wilbur?"

"I visited a spell with Willie Anderson, so I was in the vicinity, but I didn't see nor hear nothin'. Ruben kept asking, 'Did you see a car or truck on the road?' over and over like I didn't hear it the first thirty times. He wanted to jail me but he didn't have proof. After that, he accused Willie cause he was the other undesirable in the area. He stayed away from his fancy buddies."

Lexie's voice intensified, "Who do you think did it?"

"Don't know."

"Come on, Wilbur. You know everyone in those hills, and they spill their guts to you. What was the gossip?"

"Can you get me released sooner?"

"Probably not. If you testify in a murder trial, concessions are considered."

"That ain't enough."

"All I got!"

"Talk was that Cecil Lansbury killed your dad."

Lexie snapped, "Why would he?"

"Cecil and Delia got engaged. Margo stuck her nose in—again. She came up with a love note, probably from twenty years before, which said Delia was his second choice. Old Cecil got his heart broke a second time, thanks to your witch mother. Folks thought he killed your father so Margo would know what it felt like to lose the person she loved."

Lexie's chair scraped as she pushed it back, "I appreciate the information. Have the warden call me if you come up with anything else."

A guard accompanied Lexie toward the exit. A long line of shackled prisoners passed on her left. Her knees buckled, and a low moan escaped from her lips.

The burly guard steadied her, "You okay, Sheriff?"

She nodded. The prisoners continued to pass by her. The man who caused her to flounder was looking down at her. A strange darkness burned in his eyes and a faint smile curved his lips. She met his eyes, then studied his familiar face.

His stare locked on hers as he curled one side of his lip. "Take a photo, lady. It'll last longer."

The guard's words shot toward the prisoner, "Shut up, Snake, or I'll put you in solitary for a week or two."

Snake continued forward with a sneer on his lips and a sideways glance that pierced to Lexie's core.

Chapter Thirty-Three

Lexie explained the situation to Warden Brown. He agreed to a meeting with Snake in a room without a partition.

Brown shook his head. "It's probably better that you not find that one; he's as mean as his name sounds."

Lexie didn't know whether to agree or disagree, so she did neither. She called Tye, "Come get me. Car broke down at Big Mac. Mechanic said it'll be three days before it's fixed."

"Clay just got here. I'll leave within twenty minutes."

The three-hour wait seemed like an eternity. Lexie wished she'd found her nephew somewhere other than a prison. *At least the search was over.*

Snake looked like a hardened criminal. She couldn't wait to see the look on her pissy nephew's face when he learned that a sheriff was his Aunt.

Their faces were the same, but Snake's head was shaven clean. Adam's hair was cut short and swept to the side. Both had Jamie's hair color and the earthen skin shade of their father.

Tye pushed through the doorway followed by a guard. "You ready to go, Sis? I didn't plan on searching for you. Come on before your free ride leaves without you."

"I decided to wait here."

"Why are you acting weird?"

Lexie's tone softened, "I found something for you."

Tye blurted, "In a prison?"

"Your son is here!"

The big man sank into a chair, "Snake is here?"

"Yes, for attempted murder. Warden described him as 'hard as nails.' The chip on Snake's shoulder is so big, a two pound rock would fit."

"Did you tell Snake about me?"

"No, that's your job."

Tye rubbed his temples, "A son in prison—nothing gets much worse."

"He's still our blood. I won't stay long. I want to observe his reaction when he finds out his long lost aunt is a sheriff."

The guard arrived with the sulky prisoner. He was a couple of inches taller than his dad, built more like Tye than his slender twin.

"You again," Snake snarled toward Lexie.

"Yes, me!"

Tye was struck silent, so Lexie continued, "You look like the guy we've been looking for in Diffee, Oklahoma."

"Never heard of the place, much less been there. I ain't your guy. Only in Oklahoma once, and they stuck me in this prison for defending myself against a drunken fool."

"I'm sure you're the one. You know a man named Alex Thomas?"

Anger oozed from his eyes and his chin jutted forward. "I lived with the demon most of my life, then I ran off."

Probably be good to quit messing with him before he decided to assault his aunt, Lexie decided.

Tye finally found words, "What's your real name, son?"

"I named myself Brody Toms, and I ain't your son."

"Well, Brody, you are my son, and this woman is your Aunt Lexie."

"WHAT THE HELL!" Brody slammed his metal restraint against the wall. "Why did they let you crazy people in here?"

Lexie squeezed Tye's shoulder, then signaled the guard to let her out.

Chapter Thirty-Four

Tye pulled a photo from his wallet. "This is your twin brother. His name is Adam."

Brody eyeballed the photo. His rock hard stance faltered. "I don't understand."

"You and your brother were put up for adoption after birth. Thomas was supposed to handle two adoptions, but he kept you."

"Where were you?"

"I wasn't told that your mother had twins until about a year ago. Since then, I've searched for you and your brother."

"My mother threw us out like bags of trash?"

"We were both seventeen. Her father didn't think she or I could handle parenthood. He thought Thomas found you both good homes."

"That was a fool's assumption." The darkness deepened in Brody's eyes. "Get out of here, man. It's too late to play daddy. My entire life was screwed because of you and yours." Brody's hands clinched so tight that his fists turned white. He bellowed, "Get me out of here."

Tye's eyes bore into the thug's face. "Brody, you're my son whether you like it or not. You might as well get used to the fact. I'm in your life for the long haul."

Brody's spit landed on the toe of Tye's boot. The guard moved forward, but Tye signaled him to stop.

"Your anger is justified. But someday you must let it go and when you do, I'll welcome my son home."

"You're nuts, man!"

"Goodbye, Brody. I'll see you in a week."

The heavy door automatically shut behind Tye. Dragging his feet, he exited the building. His hand pressed against his forehead in a useless attempt to stop the bolts of pain that assaulted his head.

Chapter Thirty-Five

Lexie waited outside Judge Marcus Simpson's chambers hoping he'd take a break between cases. At 9:15 he scurried out the door behind his bench, his robe flowed behind him. She did nothing to slow down what apparently was an emergency trip to the restroom. Soon he reappeared, straightened his robe and smoothed his white hair.

"Can you give me five minutes, Judge?"

"Make it quick. I have a full docket today."

"I've reopened the Nodin Wolfe case. The murder weapon mysteriously disappeared from the evidence box. May I have your permission to check all the boxes at the end of the alphabet to make sure it wasn't stuck in the wrong file?"

"Yes, and what else?"

"If the knife wasn't misfiled, warrants are required to search the residences of the primary suspects. Also, I want warrants to get DNA samples."

"Whatever you need." He fled into the courtroom.

Lexie wondered about Simpson's quick exit as she walked toward her office. Perhaps his retreat was due to lateness and not guilt.

Sam gave her a half-hearted wave as she passed in front of his bench. She felt guilty about taking Ruben away from his buddy. "Sam," she hollered, "let's have a talk."

Sam scurried across the street, then followed Lexie in the door.

"Okay, folks," Lexie directed, "come join me at the table. Judge Simpson gave me permission to check the files at the courthouse. I think someone stuck the murder weapon in the wrong box. So Ruben, Delia, and Sam—if you're willing to help— we'll search the file boxes. Tye, you cover the office."

Sam's face lit up, "Hey, Ruben, looks like I'm a working man, too."

Ruben extended his fist for a bump. "I barely functioned without your advice."

"Let's parade to the courthouse. Tye, you can find us in a basement with a million dust particles if you need us."

"Sounds like a dirty job," he countered.

Sam chimed, "But somebody's gotta do it."

Lexie's new deputies and her secretary had difficulty descending the steep stairs to the courthouse basement. She feared someone would end up in a pile at the bottom of them.

"We'll start at the end of the alphabet. If the knife was misplaced, the logical assumption is that it's in the Ws, or close. When you find a knife in any box, holler for Ruben and me to check."

Silence took over as the foursome concentrated on their task. Occasionally someone called out, but close examination verified the weapon wasn't the one that killed Nodin. After a short lunch, the search continued.

At 5 p.m. they kept working. At about 7 o'clock, Lexie announced, "Enough is enough. You all look like you survived a dust bunny attack. We gave it our best shot. My fear that someone stole the weapon looks like a reality."

Lexie followed the older folks to her office door. "Ruben and Delia, don't come in until ten tomorrow morning. Sam, I'll have a check for you in three days. Thanks, everyone."

*****

Home at last. The soap scrubbed off the dirt and grime, and warm water flushed it down the drain. The rinse water from her hair ran clear after two shampoos.

One last thought filled her head as it hit the pillow. *I've got to find that murder weapon.*

Chapter Thirty-Six

An early morning phone conversation with Tye included assurances that he'd arrive before eight to relieve Clay. He also gave her a quick update on Brody.

"I'll catch the judge before his day begins to get the search warrants," she told Tye.

"I'm interested in getting a summary of Dad's case the first chance you get. I'm way out of the loop with all the Brody drama."

"I'll catch you up soon. Goodbye."

Lexie took a quick shower, not sure if the one from the night before actually removed the scum. Within thirty minutes, she was at Simpson's office. She noted that his secretary looked like she had a close encounter with a few dust bunnies.

"Go on in," she whined.

"You okay, May?"

May's mouth moved close to Lexie's ear, "Someone needs to tell his majesty that my job description doesn't include crawling in the basement."

Lexie grimaced, "For sure."

Simpson called from his office, "Back so soon, Lexie?"

"I'm here for the search warrants."

He smiled, "I have a surprise for you."

"That is?"

"This morning, May checked the 'N' files downstairs. You know N for Nodin. She found the knife in a box marked Nowlin."

"Gosh, thanks, Marcus." *Does he actually think I'm stupid enough to fall for that?*

"You're welcome." He pulled a plastic bag out of the desk's side drawer.

Lexie's heart skipped beats as she stared at the Kodiak knife. It was exactly as Ruben described.

Marcus stood, "Time for court."

"I forgot to ask you yesterday if you'd officiate at Red's and my wedding. The rehearsal is the evening before."

"I'd be honored."

Lexie cheered internally for her two victories as she jogged toward her office. The murder weapon was found, and suspect Marcus agreed to attend a wedding rehearsal with Margo present. She'd get a first hand view of their interactions and reactions. It was a good day.

Lexie placed her precious parcel on the desk in front of Tye.

"This is it!" she exclaimed.

"The knife that killed our father?" Tye's hand smoothed the plastic that covered the knife.

"Yes," Lexie responded, "the knife four people looked for all day yesterday and didn't find."

Tye looked confused, "Where did it come from?"

"It mysteriously appeared when Judge Simpson sent his secretary to look in the basement early this morning. He had her check through the N files. He thought it was clever to think someone filed it under Dad's first name rather than his last."

"I assume he didn't know that the boxes were already checked?"

"I told him we were checking the boxes near the end of the alphabet."

"Sis, do you think he's the killer?"

"He's my number one suspect since his wife died soon after Margo sent her a note of Marcus' betrayal."

Tye eyed her, "No chance one of your search crew missed the box?"

"By accident or on purpose? That eats at me. Delia isn't the sort to do anything illegal, but if she thought Cecil was the murderer and she felt guilty for dumping him—maybe. I should kick myself for getting her involved."

"Forget that theory. Delia wouldn't get involved in illegal crap," Tye concluded.

"My other dilemma is the possibility the box was missed by accident. I was meticulous, but we all got tired. I don't know." She felt her exasperation rise as she contemplated the fact she may have screwed up.

"You okay with me taking off when Delia and Ruben get here? I promised Adam I'd take him to visit Brody."

"Sure, go on. I hope Brody is civilized."

Tye's shoulders seized up, "No miracle expected."

"I'm leaving for a quick trip to Tulsa when they check in. I'll hand deliver the knife to the lab. Hopefully, one of those decorative handle grooves has a hidden DNA treasure."

Chapter Thirty-Seven

The warden agreed to a face-to-face meeting between Tye and Brody with the addition of Adam. Tye helped Adam manipulate his crutches as he exited the Jeep in the prison lot.

"Do you think Brody will give me permission to write our story, Tye?"

"You shouldn't ask this visit. He was mad as a hornet the last time I was here."

Adam slumped forward on the crutches. "No offense, but I was given away, too. I'm not the target of his malice."

"That's true, but consider the fact that he may resent you. You ended up with a good life and he ended up with crap."

"I'll play it by ear," Adam muttered.

Inside the prison, the pair sat on metal chairs bolted to the floor. The table was also attached to the floor.

Brody entered the room with downcast eyes and bandied obscenities. "What you doing here, man? I told you to get lost."

Tye hammered words toward him, "I'm about as obedient as you are, Brody."

"GO AWAY!"

"I told you before, kid, I'm here to stay."

A low growl puffed Brody's lips.

"Your brother came to visit. Brody, this is Adam."

Brody surveyed his brother up and down. "So this is the twin who got the golden egg?"

Silence hung in the room until Adam spoke, "I felt like something was absent in my life. It was like a part was gone. I wonder if I missed you."

Brody's face twisted, "The missing part was your brain. Cut the shit. That sounds like psycho twin garbage."

Tye felt angry words about to shoot from his mouth. He forced himself to remain quiet.

"You're right, not logical to miss a brother I never knew existed. I brought you a book about Michael Jordan."

Brody countered, "What makes you think I like Jordan?"

"Tye told me his poster was in your room at Thomas' house."

"Demon Daddy should mind his own business. Guard, I need to take a dump. Hearing this pair makes me want to shit."

Tye glared at his son, "Good, the shit will come out your asshole, for a change, instead of your mouth."

"Are you perturbed, Daddy-o? Maybe now you'll stay away."

"Brody, my son, it has taken twenty years to get you in my life, and there's nothing that will run me off."

Brody spit toward his father, "We'll see about that."

Tye hollered as the guard escorted Brody out, "See you next week, son."

In the vehicle headed for Diffee, the cab housed two crest-fallen men.

"You were right, Tye, he won't let me write about him. He's one mean jerk. How can you have any hope?"

"I didn't, until I saw him stash the book you brought under his shirt. A small thing, but you made a minor connection. That's all the hope I needed today."

Chapter Thirty-Eight

After her Tulsa trip, Lexie decided a surprise visit to Clayton Sr., Diffee's esteemed mayor, was in order.

"What has Clay done now?" was his opening remark.

"I'm not here about your son, Mayor. I want to know what you've done."

The flat of Clayton's hand smacked the desk, "What the hell does that mean?"

"I've reopened the Nodin Wolfe case. The records indicate that you were a person of interest."

"What a waste of taxpayer money. I assure you, when you run for re-election, I'll let the electorate know how you used their money for a personal vendetta."

"Most people don't want to reside in a town with a murderer. So a few may side with me."

"Speak your piece," he snarled.

Lexie settled into a stuffed plaid chair. Its red and black fabric coordinated perfectly with Clayton's black sofa and office chair. His glass-covered desk was carved with horses. The drapes were the same fabric as the plaid chairs.

"I wish the sheriff's office had your designer." Sarcasm dripped from her words.

"Get to the point. I assume you're not here to discuss interior decorating."

"What was the relationship between you and my mother?"

"That's a left field question. I thought you were interested in your father?"

"More and more I believe that there's a connection between my mother's flirting and my dad's death."

"Flirting . . . interesting use of the word."

"What word would you use to describe my mother's behavior?"

"Heartless. She was eleven years older and married, but teased me without mercy."

"You were around thirty then?"

"Thirty and stupid enough to think she loved me. I was her joke. Called me a slobbering puppy to her snobby friends. I'm showing them now. I've reached heights they'll never touch."

"Mayor, I need a DNA sample."

"What for?"

"Fifteen years ago they didn't have the technology to match DNA. I found the murder weapon. The lab is pulling out DNA from the knife handle, probably as we speak."

Clayton commanded, "Get a court order."

Lexie whipped the form from her pocket, "A special delivery from Judge Simpson."

The Mayor cursed as she pulled on the gloves. She swabbed the inside of his cheek, then deposited the sample in a container.

His tone deflated, "That all, Sheriff?"

"Yes, that's it, thanks."

Her long strides carried her quickly from Clayton's office to Cecil's office, a block off Main Street.

"Come in," Cecil called from his desk. "Secretary out sick again. Allergies mess her up in the fall."

"Hello, Cecil."

"Got your plastic bag ready, Lexie?"

"Who ruined my surprise?"

"Ran into Marcus after court. He told me you requested my spit."

Lexie collected her sample. "Did Marcus also tell you he signed a slip, then I filled in his name?"

"We got a good laugh out of that."

"Are you attending my wedding?"

"Sorry, Lexie, don't want to be in the same state with Margo, much less the same house."

"Please reconsider. Delia would look mighty good with you on her arm."

"Delia wouldn't agree to stand that close to me."

"Thanks for your time, Cecil." *Such a good man, surely he isn't a murderer.*

Chapter Thirty-Nine

Lexie squinted at the clock—6 a.m. She forced her eyes wide open. She'd question Larry Prather this morning about her father's murder. Avoiding his work site, she decided a 7 a.m. stop at his front door was in order. An unwelcome visitor with a DNA bag was soon on the way to his place.

Her knock on the door was polite, until it got no results. Her fist attacked the door. The window in the door vibrated.

Prather growled as the door swung open. His wet hair clamped to his forehead. An old terry robe barely overlapped across his belly.

"What do you want, Lexie? I got to get to work."

"May I come in?"

"We can talk on the porch. You got info about Grass?"

"He was a dead end."

"Do you think he killed Hawk?"

"Didn't ask, not my jurisdiction."

Prather probed, "I bet you got a feel for whether or not he thought Hawk got what he deserved."

"Not my business. I want information about Dad's murder. I found out something interesting, Larry, when I looked through the file. You thought Willie Anderson was a suspect."

"Like you'd turn in your fiancé's uncle, no chance."

"I assure you, I'd lock the cell and throw away the key if he had anything to do with the death."

"I saw Willie on the road that day. That's all—no proof that fingered him."

"What were you doing on the road?"

"As you well know, I traveled that way to and from my house."

Lexie pointed a finger, "Did you try to pin the murder on Willie to distract Ruben from the real culprit?"

Larry fired back, "You're as big a bitch as your mother."

"Why was my mother a bitch, Larry?"

"No business of yours," he grumbled.

"It's my business if she made you so angry you paid her back."

"Get lost. I got work."

She caught his arm as he reached for the knob, "And I get a DNA sample before you leave."

His eyes examined her face while she brushed the swab inside his cheek. Goose bumps formed on her arms. The unexplained anxiety appeared out of nowhere. She backed up and almost tripped over a sleeping hound.

His eyes were on her as she walked away. She felt like an insect under a microscope. *What was that about?*

Chapter Forty

It was an uneventful workday, with the exception of the creepiness she'd felt around Prather. At quitting time she left to meet Red at their home-to-be. She pondered her dilemma. To lie or not to lie was the question. Not really lie–just avoid the truth.

Since Willie's DNA wasn't available, a sample from Red would result in a familial match if Willie were guilty. *How does one tell her fiancé that his uncle may be a murderer? Red's DNA might send his uncle to prison, or worse.*

If she waited for the sample until after Willie arrived for the wedding, he'd leave before the results got back. If she didn't tell Red the truth, he wouldn't go ballistic over the request. She still hadn't decided what to do by the time she arrived in the living room of their home.

Red's arms wrapped around her and he kissed her on the forehead and cheeks. Then his lips landed on hers for a very good minute.

"Glad to see you, too, husband-to-be."

"Wife-to-be, let's decide the living room arrangement for the wedding. Does the downstairs need furnished ASAP?"

"We can wait on the furniture. We'll borrow fold-up chairs from the church so we can seat more people."

"Great idea," Red agreed.

"Have you decided what you, Tye, and Adam are wearing?"

"Black suits with white shirts."

Lexie pinched his cheek, "I knew I'd never get you two in tuxedos."

"I never related well to penguins."

She smoothed his cheek, "Will you sing to me during the wedding?"

"I love you, woman, but I can't handle singing in front of all those people."

"Cluck, cluck, cluck."

"Yep, I'm a chicken. I found two used bedroom sets at the Furniture Hut that look good. You can pick us out a new set for the master bedroom. My old set is in the fourth bedroom where I sleep."

"Sounds like the house is almost ready for our big day. Let's go to Dixie's for supper."

"No can do. Got a late flight today. Some guy decided he wanted to gamble in Tunica, and he's paying double. I took the job because I heard wives are very expensive. "

Lexie wrapped her arms around him. "I'll lock up. I'll measure our bedroom and decide on pieces. Love you!"

"Love you, too."

She climbed the stairs to Red's bathroom. She retrieved a plastic glove from her purse, then pulled a strand of red hair off a comb and sealed the bag.

All the way home she chastised herself. She should have told him, but there was no reason he had to know. If he'd said no, she would've taken his DNA anyway. What was that old saying, 'easier to get forgiveness than permission?'

Chapter Forty-One

Tye drove toward Big Mac, his mind intent on Jamie's first meeting with Brody. He'd put her off for eight weeks. He feared that Brody's hostility would intensify the guilt she already felt. She no longer listened to his reasons to stay away. Jamie insisted on meeting the monster they created.

Tye remembered her face and tears the day Adam forgave her. He didn't expect forgiveness today— only the regular flow of hate from Brody's mouth.

"What are you thinking about, Tye?"

"I don't think you have any idea what you're getting into?"

Tears filled her eyes, "I must see him for myself."

"I've visited him once a week for almost two months and he's like a frozen pond, hard, from the hate that stiffened inside of him."

"You've given up?"

"Sometimes, but then a little hope reappears." Tye parked at the far end of the lot. The couple walked silently toward the entry.

Tye addressed the guard, "We're here to see Brody Toms."

The guard grimaced.

Tye clarified, "Better known as Snake."

"Snake was shipped out yesterday."

Tye's words choked out, "What? Where to?"

"Talk to the warden."

Warden Brown frowned when Tye and Jamie entered his office. "Have a seat."

"No thanks. Where's Brody?"

Brown's voice boomed, "Since his time here was about up, we let him go."

Tye's body stiffened, "You let him go?" Restrained anger crept out with his question. "You knew I searched for him for months and you didn't even notify me. Now I have to start over?"

Venom mixed with Brown's words, "I don't run a social club here. Anyway, I know where he is. He's where he belongs, in a prison in Nevel, Kansas, charged with the murder of Alex Thomas."

Thirty minutes later, Tye stared straight ahead as he drove toward home. The gray day was turning to a black night. Tree limbs were skeletons of autumn. They were left bare by the winter wind that stripped them of their colorful leaves a month before.

The scarf Jamie pressed against her face absorbed soft sobs.

Guilt burned in his body and sweat soaked into his shirt. His DNA sample must have traced the murder back to Brody. An act, meant to find his son, inadvertently resulted in a murder charge. Adding to his sorrow was the fact that his son was more than capable of killing Thomas. Not even a fragment of hope remained.

Chapter Forty-Two

Lexie settled into her old desk chair. A hurried morning trip to Tulsa to deliver DNA samples left her consumed with 'what if?' scenarios. The worst one: "What if Red's uncle was the killer?"

The back door banged against the wall, which overwhelmed the monotonous ticking of the clock. Clay's feet slammed the floor with each step. The lines on his face formed a map of contained hatred. His hand shook as he pointed at Lexie, "You accused my father of murder to back-stab me."

"No, Clay, I'm investigating your father because he was identified sixteen years ago as a person of interest."

"Damn you to hell!"

"Glad you don't have that power." Lexie controlled the smile that tempted her lips.

"You better not hurt my dad."

"I understand how you feel. I'm defending my dad, also. I'll investigate anyone and anything related to his murder. So shut up and get out until it's time for work."

Clay's long strides carried him out the back door. His farewell slam sent a wave of anger through Lexie. She should fire him, but not now. It'd look like harassment to punish Clayton.

A creak from the front door announced her next visitor. He came softly across the room, it was like an apparition joined her. He reached out a packet with the word *Resume* typed on the top page.

"I'm Sheriff Lexie Wolfe."

He focused on her face, "John Jackson."

"What can I do for you, John?"

"I want a job. Got a background in law enforcement from Mississippi."

"Why didn't you stay in Mississippi?"

"Time for a change."

"Hmm," Lexie scanned the first couple of pages. "Looks like you have experience."

"I'm a hard worker and don't mind long hours."

"With little pay?" Lexie smiled.

John's austere appearance remained, "Enough to get by."

"That coincides with the Diffee budget."

John's frown remained frozen in place.

"No funds until January," Lexie stated. "If you're still available, I'll interview you next month. Can you wait that long for a job?"

John's lips barely moved, "I'll be back."

He exited without parting words. Lexie figured she'd have to put a bell on a deputy who was that quiet and moved so stealthily.

She wasn't fooled by John's quietness or the softness of his movement. The darkness in his eyes and the hardness in his demeanor revealed a man who had faced tough times. However, he was the deputy she needed—few words—hard as nails.

Lexie rose from her chair as soon as Delia returned from lunch. "Unfortunately, it is time to meet my mom."

Delia piped up, "Glad it's you and not me."

Chapter Forty-Three

Lexie waited at the fork in the highway. She planned to intercept Margo before she ended up at Loretta's. Not sure where to take her mother. The office didn't work since Delia was there. Margo would verbally beat the crap out of Lexie's living environment. Her final decision was to have Margo follow to Lexie's home-to-be.

Earlier, she attempted to find an outfit that her mom wouldn't belittle. As it turned out, there was no Margo-approved apparel in her closet. She decided on a classic, white long-sleeved shirt and blue jeans. She successfully put her hair up.

Lexie honked when a black Cadillac stopped at the sign. She'd texted Margo earlier so she knew to follow. After leaving the blacktop, the ride was dusty for a few miles. Every once in a while, Margo honked and threw her hands up as if to say, 'Where in the hell are you taking me?'

Lexie pulled in front of the house. She pledged that she wouldn't cut out Margo's tongue even if she insulted Red's work.

"Lexie, look at my car. Your road trip could've waited until after my visit to Loretta's. My car is filthy."

"Country living, Mom. It's a dirt road to Loretta's, also."

"I don't know how I ever survived out in the boonies," Margo griped.

"Come in, Mom. I'm proud of all Red did to fix this place up."

"My goodness, it looks good. His father didn't have Red's talent for renovation."

"You've been in this house?"

"Of course. Red's mom and I attended school together way back when. Is she attending the wedding?"

"No, she's in poor health. She doesn't travel long distances."

"That sage trim on your house is so two years ago, but it still looks nice."

Lexie clamped her lips and opened the front door.

"No furniture?"

"We can seat more people using the church folding chairs. We'll furnish the house after the wedding."

Margo swiped her hand across a chair seat. "The fold-up chairs look dingy."

Lexie gripped a chair back. "I went over them once, and that's all I have time for."

"That's too bad."

"Come upstairs, Mom. I want you to see my new bedroom set."

Margo followed at a record slow pace. "Lovely. Did you pick this out yourself?"

Lexie rolled her eyes, "No, I called the editor of *House Beautiful* for advice."

Margo scolded, "You and your sarcasm. I hoped you'd outgrow it."

"I have inspiration to continue."

"I bet you do in that man-job of yours."

Mom missed the point yet again. "Let's sit at the kitchen table. I bought croissant sandwiches and fruit cups from the bakery for lunch."

Lexie pulled out a chair, "See the carving on the back?"

"Wonderful, looks professional."

Lexie glanced at her mother as she chewed. Many thought her mom resembled Elizabeth Taylor. Margo was a petite woman with a perfectly proportioned figure. Her black, chin-length hair fell in soft curls. A gentleness and vulnerability radiated from her—until she opened her mouth. Lexie understood how a man could fall victim to her mother's charm and beauty.

Margo pushed her half-finished plate aside, "We girls better watch our figures." She eyed Lexie's empty plate.

Lexie's posture straightened, "I've reopened Dad's case. I have questions that require answers."

Margo's words erupted, "NO, I'm not talking about that! I came here to enjoy a wedding, not talk about things that are dead and buried."

"They aren't dead to me."

"Give it up, Lexie. It was a drifter who robbed us and killed your father. You're wasting my time and yours."

Lexie ignored Margo's rant, "I asked questions around town. I heard about men who were attracted to you. Men who might kill to get your husband out of the way."

A crooked smile formed on Margo's red lips. "Yes, there were a few who desired me beyond sanity."

"Men who were insane enough to kill Dad?"

"Any of them . . . but none of them, according to Ruben's investigation," she sniped.

"Why is Larry Prather vindictive toward me? He was only seventeen or eighteen back then. Surely he wasn't in love with you, or did you seduce him, too?"

Margo's face reddened, "Instead of hateful words, you should thank me. He thought I'd let someone from his no-good family date you. I told him in no uncertain terms that no Prather trash was getting near my daughter."

No wonder he hates me. Lexie's hands trembled as she controlled the explosion brewing inside. With great willpower she flattened the tone of her voice. "I have a list of things you said were stolen. It includes the opal ring you're wearing on your right hand. How did you get it back?"

Margo's bottom lip quivered, "I lied for the insurance money. I owed three thousand on your facial surgery, and Nodin's funeral cost over five thousand."

Lexie fanned the fire, "Did you lie about the other items on the list?"

"I did, and I don't regret it one bit. I needed that money," she shrieked.

"You're admitting nothing was stolen? Nothing taken but my father's life?"

"Don't be judgmental. It was your fault I lied to the insurance company. If you'd gone shopping with me, you wouldn't have gotten knifed. You left me saddled with all those medical bills because you're so damn stubborn."

"Who was obsessed enough to kill for you: Cecil, Marcus, Willie, Clayton, or someone else?"

"They were country bumpkins. All of them would've killed to have me. Good luck finding the right man. I'm leaving for Loretta's. God only knows why I didn't have a delightful daughter like her instead of someone who has no respect for her mother."

"Too bad is right," Lexie mumbled.

"I'll return tomorrow for the wedding rehearsal and spend the night. Wedding or no wedding, if you mention the murder again, I'll walk out the door and leave you without a hostess."

The slammed door echoed through the living room into the kitchen. Lexie rested her head on the table. Tears made paths down her cheeks, not because she wasn't the daughter her mother wanted. Her tears fell for the mother she never had.

Chapter Forty-Four

Lexie punched the Tulsa Lab number into her phone.

"Results aren't conclusive," Bryce reported. "I'm checking every indentation in the knife handle: no luck so far."

"One of my suspects will leave after my wedding on Saturday. Your results may catch a killer."

"Doing the best I can. Had a couple of bigwig fatalities. My boss made me push back your case. Frankly, he thinks your investigation is futile and self-serving."

"Would you think so if it was your father, Bryce?"

"No. I'll keep searching," he promised.

"Thanks."

Chapter Forty-Five

The breeze ruffled her hair as she drove toward her future home. The weather forecaster had confused winter with spring. The December day was clear with an expected high of sixty-seven. The sun was as bright as Lexie's spirit.

When she arrived, she surveyed the living room. The folding chairs were set in neat rows. Pots of red poinsettias balanced the area with color. Single silk poinsettias were woven into the pine garlands that curved down the bannisters on either side of the staircase she'd descend to reach her groom.

Dixie was catering the evening rehearsal. Margo instructed her on the preparation of finger food that wealthy people consumed. Margo found fine wine and the correctly shaped glasses in Tulsa. Lexie hadn't a clue that it mattered. Margo complained loudly when told there was no time or money for a sit down dinner.

Red's father, Kurt, and Uncle Willie hadn't arrived due to a flight delay into Tulsa.

Her cell phone rang out the Rocky theme, "Sheriff Wolfe here."

"It's Bryce. Finally got results."

Lexie held her breath, "What?"

"Results indicated DNA from three men. One is Marcus Simpson, the second is a familial match to Red Anderson, and the third is your dad."

Lexie sucked in as much air as her lungs could handle. "Thanks." *The worst was happening.*

A car engine out front indicated that she'd soon welcome the cause of her apprehension. A shiver went through her body as she opened the door. Red wrapped his arm around her shoulders. "Dad, you remember Lexie. Uncle Willie, have you met her?"

"I saw her around when she was a kid. I knew her dad."

She gave each man a quick hug. Her nose caught on a sickening scent that churned her stomach and tightened her chest.

Kurt's hair had one streak of auburn that somehow survived the color transformation to gray over the years. His shoulders bent forward. He looked older than his sixty-five years.

Uncle Willie was probably six years younger. His wild gray hair reminded Lexie of a mad professor she'd seen on television. A hairy face camouflaged his facial structure. *Did his green eyes convey a mischievous glint, or was that evil?*

"Red, please get them settled. I have an errand in town before everyone shows up."

Lexie restrained from floor-boarding the gas as she sped toward the courthouse. She wanted Marcus Simpson's statement before he arrived for the rehearsal. He picked up his briefcase as Lexie barged through his door, "Let's talk, Marcus."

"Expected you before this. That lab must be moving slow on results."

"You know your DNA is on the weapon?"

"Yes," he confirmed.

"Do you think my mother hurting your wife's feelings was just cause to kill my father?"

"I didn't kill Nodin."

Lexie paced, "That's not what the evidence says. Your DNA is on the weapon that you snuck into the box. Why didn't you wipe it clean?"

"I took it home for my knife collection years ago. I didn't think there was any harm since the case was closed. When you started looking for it, I put it in the N file. Not appropriate for a judge to confiscate evidence."

"Especially doesn't look good when you're a prime suspect!"

His eyes avoided Lexie's belligerent stare. "If I was guilty, I would've wiped the weapon clean. I'll head home and clean up before your wedding rehearsal." Simpson's arm brushed against her as he exited.

Was he playing me? Did he hire Willy to kill Nodin?

Chapter Forty-Six

Lexie stopped by home to put on the royal blue dress Margo bought during a shopping spree with Loretta. She hated to admit it, but the dress was gorgeous; slim style with a slightly folded neck and long sleeves. She brushed out her hair and used the curling iron to add body. A gold barrette held her hair to one side.

The make-up base Margo bought to cover the scar actually worked pretty well, even though its purchase was an obvious insult. Looking in the mirror, she barely recognized herself. The sheriff was camouflaged, except for eyes that revealed a worried mind.

Tonight she'd enjoy time with Red. She'd concentrate on finding the murderer later.

Lexie's eyes surveyed a sparkling array of lights as she came within sight of her new home. Red had put clear Christmas lights around the eaves and down all the perimeters of the house. The place looked like a fantasy destination.

He waited on the porch, "I was getting worried. Everyone else is here."

"I'm right on time for my grand entrance. Give me a courage booster." She kissed him hard on the lips. "I'm powered up. Let's go face our relatives."

"I'll power you up any time, girl. By the way, you look drop dead beautiful."

"Thank you, kind sir."

Arm in arm they entered the room. She surveyed the familiar faces: Adam, Tye, Jamie, Beth, Margo, Kurt, Loretta, Willie and the Judge. Delia was a no-show.

Margo squeezed close, "You look good when you try. That make-up and new dress make all the difference in the world."

"Come on, slow pokes," Loretta ordered. "Jamie, Beth, Lexie, get to the top of the stairs. Let's get this practice over before the food sets too long."

Multiple eyes stared as Lexie walked down the steps. Margo called from below, "Pull those shoulders back, and keep your eyes fixed on Red."

Lexie tried to look straight ahead. Concern about falling on her head averted her eyes downward every other step.

The practice over, hostess Margo and Loretta took over the festivities. Kenny G's CD played softly in the background. All the food was arranged on beautiful cut glass platters that matched the punch bowl and cups. A bouquet of white roses served as the centerpiece on a royal blue tablecloth. She hoped Margo didn't hand her a bill for all the finery.

Lexie watched the guests interact. Grandpa used to talk about 'walking on egg shells,' which was an appropriate description of the group. Tye and Red were the only males who went near Margo. When she came close, the other men averted their eyes to a picture, the floor, or the closest face that didn't belong to her. Margo's smiles and greetings were met with a nod and avoidance. Once, Lexie caught Simpson staring at Margo. His neck reddened when he saw Lexie's eyes on him. Willie and the judge had no interactions.

Social time completed, the atmosphere was so subdued that she pulled Tye aside. "Will you toast these people out the door?"

Tye held his glass high, "I'm ending this party with a toast to a life of happiness for my best friend and my sister."

"Thank you, Mom," Lexie added, "for providing all the food and decorations for our rehearsal dinner. You're a fantastic hostess." Lexie noted Margo's stunned expression. *Likely the hostess didn't plan to pay for her expensive taste.*

Chapter Forty-Seven

Lexie accompanied Margo to a third floor bedroom. "I thought it went well, Mom. I was concerned that your old admirers might verbally tangle."

Margo's lips spread into a pleased smile. "Perhaps they've learned to control themselves over the years."

"Goodnight, Mom."

Lexie paused on the stairs at the second floor. Willie and Kurt were housed on opposite ends of the hall. She admitted to herself that she wanted a show of anger from one of the guests. A murderer who verbally attacked Margo for a life of guilt would've solved her dad's case.

When she reached the main floor, she found Red finishing a beer. She told him earlier she'd spend the night at her own place, but she fibbed. "Go to bed, Red. I've decided to rearrange the chairs."

"I'll help."

"No, thanks. I'll do my woman thing. Think about it for ten minutes, then change my mind five times. Get some rest, man. After tonight you'll be a husband, and I hear that's hard work."

She kissed the middle of his forehead while standing on her tiptoes. She pulled away from his touch.

His bottom lip protruded, "Since this is my last night as a single man, I deserve a better kiss. Good motivation to get me through the ceremony tomorrow."

"Dream on, mister. Get to bed." She gave his butt a pat when he turned.

"Hey girl, stay away from my private parts. I'm almost a married man!"

Their laughter merged as he ascended the stairs. At the top he put his hand on his lips and threw her a kiss. Lexie caught it and touched her lips.

"I love you, and tomorrow will be the best day of my life." A few seconds passed as he looked down at her, apparently waiting for a reply.

"No comment." She grinned.

She rearranged six chairs, retrieved her bag from the hall closet, then headed for the bathroom.

The warm shower water soothed the evening tension. Amber Romance gel filled her nostrils with the loveliest of smells as she spread it over her body.

She dried her hair, then pulled the white silk, floor-length, nightgown over her head. Her hair fell to her waist when she released it from the barrette. A touch of lip-gloss, and she was ready to seduce the redheaded man upstairs.

Her feet barely touched each step as she climbed upwards. Quietly she opened the door; only a creak interrupted the silence.

Red's side lamp came on as he stirred to find the sound's source.

She crawled in beside him, "I love you, too." As soon as she got in, he rolled out the other side. She remained silent and watched.

He took his guitar from the corner and sat on the end of the bed. His strummed as his emotions came through a poem's words.

> Light of my life
> Elusive dream
> I waited for you
>
> Now it is time
> Take my heart
> Give me yours
>
> Hold me tonight
> Joined in love
> I'll know it's real
>
> Dreams became truth
> Tomorrow you're mine
> Our wedding day

*****

Her breathing merged with the poem's rhythm.

Finished, he returned to the bedside and pulled the white gown over her head. He stopped, and his eyes examined her. A whisper of love in her ear, then gentle kisses on her face, throat, breasts and belly took her breath away.

She kissed him passionately, their tongues conveyed a message that words never adequately expressed. She ran her fingers through the red hair on his chest and beyond. Her face pressed against his neck, kissing him time after time.

Their passion increased with each soft or firm touch. She hugged him tightly as if to never let him go. His tender touch allowed her body to move freely with the waves of their love.

They lay quietly after. Their sweaty bodies intertwined for a goodnight kiss before they fell asleep.

Chapter Forty-Eight

The quiet swish of a door opening, then the alternate falling of feet in the hall outside the bedroom brought Lexie's body to attention. She rolled from the bed, pulled on panties and Red's T-shirt.

She slipped the Sig 220 from her bag and walked softly to the door. The rhythmic tune of Red's breathing didn't falter. Pulling the door shut behind her, she followed the sound that crept up the stairs.

Lexie paused midway. This gave the night stalker the chance to reach his destination. If she heard Willie confess to her father's murder, the case was solved. Patience was a necessity.

The bedroom door banged as the knob hit the wall. The moan of Margo's voice was clearly audible, "GET THE HELL OUT OF HERE!"

"I loved you, Margo, and you left me. I killed Nodin for nothing." He aimed the gun.

Margo's scream pierced the air.

Lexie ran through the doorway and tackled Willie from the back. His gun flew into the air and the murderer landed flat on his face. He struggled to sitting.

Lexie gasped for air, then "KURT!" exploded out.

Red huffed in the doorway, "What's wrong?"

Strength drained from her body. She uttered words without feeling. "Your father killed mine."

His face whitened, "That not true."

"He admitted it."

Red's eyes darkened, "You're wrong."

"I have a DNA match."

"That's impossible. He's not been here long enough to test." His eyes rammed visual daggers into her face. His words rolled out in a raspy croak, "You used my DNA?"

"I searched for a familial match to your uncle. I didn't think your father was the murderer. Willie was the suspect."

"Get that crazy creep out of here," Margo screeched.

Kurt lunged toward Margo, "Evil shrew, you destroyed my life."

Red's hand grasped Kurt's shoulder, then pulled him back.

"The witch must die!"

Lexie pointed her gun at Kurt, "Let's go downstairs."

Willie met them on the steps, "What the hell?"

"Your brother is a murdering fool," Margo yelled.

"Shut up, she-devil!" Willie shouted back.

Lexie ordered, "Grab the handcuffs from my bag, Red."

"I won't participate in my father's entrapment."

"Mom, get the handcuffs."

Margo whimpered, "After all this abuse, you expect me to run errands?"

"This once keep your mouth shut and cooperate," Lexie pleaded.

Margo retrieved the handcuffs, and then joined Lexie on the first floor.

Lexie looped the metal ring around the staircase rail. Kurt moaned and growled like a rabid animal as she locked him to the railing.

Red sat beside him on the step, "Why, Dad?"

"I did it for Margo. She said that Nodin kept us apart. I killed him for us."

Margo's face twisted in rage, "You fool, I didn't tell you to kill him. I thought you'd go away if you realized I wasn't leaving my husband."

"You wanted him dead. I knew you loved me by the way you smiled at me and touched my hand when no one was looking."

"I felt sorry for you. Pitiful the way you drooled over me. I didn't want my husband dead."

"You said that Lexie wouldn't be home."

The vase sprang from Margo's hand and hurled toward Kurt's head. With one raised fist, Red redirected the vase to the floor. Glass fragments sprayed around them.

Lexie's words punctured the air, "Get out of here, Margo."

As she ascended the steps, Kurt grabbed her ankle. "I loved you more than life."

Margo fell forward. Her scream ripped through the room. "Get that animal away from me!"

Red pulled Kurt's clenched fingers off her ankle.

She crawled up three steps, then used the banister to stand.

"Go out the back," Lexie ordered.

Margo obeyed with a shut mouth.

"Let my father go home, Lexie," Red pleaded.

Her tone was soft, "You know I can't."

"Yes, you can—for me."

"I'm the sheriff," she said flatly.

"Quit right now. Let him go–for me," Red begged.

Her contained anger rose to the surface, "He's a murderer. He'll rot in prison for my father's death."

Anger saturated Red's words, "Your witch mother egged him on."

"The knife was in his hand, not hers."

"It was she as much as him, and you know it," Red stormed.

Lexie started punching Tye's number into her phone.

Willie grabbed her from behind. The unexpected movement, from the man who stood silent during the entire ordeal, took Lexie by surprise. He wrapped his arm around her neck; the human vise slowly tightened.

Red squeezed her hand until the phone dropped. He ransacked her pocket for the handcuff key.

As soon as Kurt was released, he jumped from his perch on the steps and stumbled forward.

"Dad, wait!"

Kurt's pace quickened, as he disappeared out the front door.

With the distraction in process, Willie's grip loosened. She grabbed a handful of his hair with her left hand. Her right-hand nails scratched down the side of his face. His hold slackened long enough for her to pull away from the vise on her neck.

Red grabbed her arm as she struggled. She furiously kicked, hitting Willie's ankle, then Red's knee. Willie careened to the floor when her fist hit his face. Red's arms wrapped around her waist and lifted. Her legs kicked wildly. With his balance compromised, he fell to the floor with Lexie in his grip.

Willie held the retrieved gun to her head.

Red huffed out words, "What are you doing, man?"

"Giving Kurt time. Handcuff her to the stair rail."

Red clamped the squirming woman.

"I thought you loved me, Red Anderson."

"You're a conniving bitch. Stole my DNA to condemn my father. You're for sure your mother's daughter."

The anger rose inside, then burst violently out her mouth. "I'm my father's daughter! Kurt took him from me! Sooner or later he'll fry or rot in prison!"

Chapter Forty-Nine

Tye rolled over to retrieve the cell phone. The irritating buzz interrupted a sound sleep.

"Tye, Tye, those crazy men hurt me," Margo sobbed. "Lexie is alone with them."

He tried to make sense of her ramblings. "What are you talking about, Mom?"

"Save Lexie," she cried.

"Where is she?"

"At Red's house."

"Isn't Red with her?"

Margo whimpered, "He's so angry, he may kill her."

"He's supposed to marry her today, Mom."

"There will be no wedding. Lexie found out Red's dad killed your father."

"Oh God, no!" Tye felt his chest tighten. His words huffed out with his contained breath, "Where are you?"

"I'm at Loretta's."

Tye pushed the off button, pulled on his jeans and T-shirt. He grabbed his gun and ran out the door.

The old Jeep that replaced his demolished truck refused to go over sixty-five. Disconnected fragments of despair filled his brain. *How was this possible? This was supposed to be the happiest day for his sister and best friend. Now it was a nightmare.*

Upon arrival, he saw that the two upper stories revealed lit interiors. One lone light was visible inside the front room. Tye walked to the side window and peered in. Lexie sat on a stair step. Her right arm lifted to the handrail where a handcuff held her. Red was nowhere in sight. Tye walked to the front door and quietly turned the knob. His old boots squeaked as he attempted to enter the room quietly.

Lexie cried out, "Unlock me!"

"What happened?" Tye struggled to insert the retrieved key into the lock.

Lexie's words spilled out, "Kurt killed Dad. Red and Willie handcuffed me so Kurt could escape."

"Where are they?"

"I guess they went after Kurt. I heard Willie tell Red that all the vehicles were still parked. Kurt must have left on foot."

The front door crashed open sending waves of sound throughout the house. The only light in the room hit Red's face. Pallid skin drenched in tears surrounded hate-embedded eyes.

"Come," he ordered.

Lexie followed him toward the barn with Tye straggling behind.

She followed Red's eyes as his gaze rose to the rafters. His father's limp body hung from a roughly knotted rope. Kurt had swung a rope over a rafter from the loft of the barn. One knot held the rope in place. The other one held the loop firmly around Kurt's throat when he had stepped from the loft into the air.

Red's eyes met Lexie's and his words stabbed into the silence, "A Father for a Father."

Chapter Fifty

Lexie watched as Tye climbed the loft ladder three rungs at a time. He pulled the loop that held Kurt's body across the wood beam toward himself, untied the knot and lowered the body to Red.

Red's arms held his father as if he were a fallen child. Lexie felt sorrow whirl in the air around the men. She turned toward the double barn door and walked out into the morning air. The sun streaked the house with light. This was where they were to share a life and raise a family.

She made calls from the front porch swing: first the Highway Patrol to investigate, then the medical examiner, next the funeral home to transport the body, and Delia last.

"Delia, it's Lexie."

"What's wrong? You sound terrible."

"A long story. Phone everyone on the wedding list. Tell them the wedding is cancelled. Red's father died this morning."

"Dear God! I'm so sorry this happened on your wedding day. I'll tell folks you'll reschedule soon."

"We won't reschedule."

"I don't understand, Lexie."

"I can't talk now. Please, make the calls."

"Of course, of course," Delia stuttered.

Lexie studied the vehicles parked near the house. Willie's rental was gone. *I bet he took off in an attempt to save his skin.* Three hours passed while she answered questions, then she sat alone as the investigators did their work.

The sun was sinking when the hearse pulled up near the barn. Its human cargo was loaded, and the driver moved down the road. She visualized Red sitting on the dirt floor inside the barn, a broken man. Red's love turned to hate.

Back inside the house, she retrieved her bag and clothes. She'd ask Delia and Jamie to collect the wedding stuff. She pulled her wedding dress from the closet and smoothed the white satin before slinging the dress over her shoulder.

Lexie looked in the hall mirror as she exited. Her hand traced the scar on her cheek. She spoke to the sad reflection, "I got your killer, Daddy."

Chapter Fifty-One

Lexie lay in the crumpled bed: her chosen refuge. Two months had passed since the holocaust of her life and she couldn't shake the dark world that engulfed her emotions.

The wedding dress hung from the top of the bedroom door. The first month, tears always blurred its presence. Lately, she petted it softly and fingered the beadwork with clear vision. Perhaps that meant the depression had lifted. Clay told her that Red flew off right after his father's body was sent home.

After undergoing interrogation related to her possible role in Nodin's murder, Margo left for Dallas in a rage. Kurt was dead and there was no proof that Margo was an accessory to murder so the case was dropped.

Others packed the wedding paraphernalia. Delia made sure Lexie didn't have to deal with anything.

Lexie didn't neglect her job, but her life and work were merely burdens to bear. Delia worried about her weight loss, but Lexie argued that ten pounds wasn't that much. Food had lost all its appeal.

She'd fulfilled her promise. After all these years, her father's killer had paid for what he had done. Her goal was accomplished, even though she had never imagined the high price of revenge.

When she heard the Sunday paper hit the front door, she considered getting up, but decided against it. Off work until tomorrow, she would stay in bed and study the crack in the ceiling above her bed.

Chapter Fifty-Two

Tye walked up the steps to Paula's front door. The door swung open before he knocked. Gabriel welcomed him with a big grin.

Tye hollered to Paula, "It's me."

Two backpacks sat beside the sofa. A truck and a ball leaned up against each. "Who's leaving?" he asked Paula.

"I guess you haven't heard," she replied. "These boys have a new daddy."

"Good grief, I hope he's a good one."

"Will you still come see us?" Seth asked.

"Please," Gabriel begged.

Tye sat on the floor. The boys immediately cuddled into the crooks of his arms. "No, I won't visit your new daddy."

A tear escaped from Gabriel's eye. Seth pulled away, but Tye tugged back.

"I can't visit your new daddy because I'm your new daddy."

"You are?" Seth's eyes rounded.

"That's me! I filled out a million papers and went to Good Daddy School." Tye squashed his boys into a three-male hug.

Chapter Fifty-Three

When he arrived home with the boys, Jamie's car was parked out front. She had purchased chicken for their first family dinner. Tye carried the toys while the boys lugged their backpacks.

"Welcome home," Jamie called as she opened the door.

Tye pointed, "Boys, take the stuff to your room."

They stood at the door side-by-side, staring at their new room. Tan Berber carpet covered the floor. Blue bedspreads with red, green, and yellow airplanes decorated each twin bed. Three toy airplanes were hanging suspended from the ceiling.

"The red chest-of-drawers is yours, Seth. The blue one is Gabriel's. The yellow toy box is to share."

Gabriel opened the box and peered inside, "Come look, Seth."

Soon the fire station, police station and garage were situated around the room.

Tye loitered in the kitchen, "Need any help?"

"How are they doing?" she asked.

"Playing like they've lived here forever. I appreciate you decorating the boys' room."

"I enjoyed it."

Tye took a deep breath, "Do you think you'd have time to help me with the boys once in a while?"

"No."

His response was rapid fire, "I understand, you've got your own life. I shouldn't have asked."

Jamie called to the guys, "Come and eat."

After a short prayer, they attacked their chicken legs and macaroni and cheese.

Tye knew he was too quiet, but Jamie's abrupt 'no' was an unexpected slap in the face. Much to his chagrin, she brought it up again in front of the boys.

"As I said, I don't want to help with these boys once in a while." She slid from her chair and knelt on one knee. "Tye Wolfe, will you marry me and allow me to help you take care of your boys all the time?"

One tear escaped before his macho ego stopped it. "Yes, I'll be your husband."

He pulled Jamie up and kissed her amidst the smell of fried chicken and the clapping of small hands.

"We'll marry you, too!" Gabriel announced with conviction.

Epilogue
Seven Months Later

Lexie was nearly asleep when the phone rang beside her. "What's happening, Tye?"

"Wanted to let you know that the jury went out a few minutes ago. It may be an hour or a week or more before they determine Brody's fate. Sorry I'm in Kansas instead of with you."

"That's where you belong."

"I suppose."

"What's wrong, Tye? You sound depressed. Do you think Brody will be convicted?"

"I think he'll get released because of the abuse Thomas inflicted on him for years."

Lexie was silent for a few seconds. "You don't want him acquitted?"

"I don't know. At the least, he's mean, at the most, evil. I can't wrap my head around bringing a murderer to Diffee to live with my family."

"Phone me as soon as you find out something."

"Will do. Later."

The soft whimper from the bassinet beside Lexie was her call to pick up the tiny girl. Lori Sky Anderson didn't need to be held at that moment, but her mommy loved to look at her sky blue eyes and that baldhead with wisps of red hair. Lexie counted fingers and toes for the second time since the birth a few hours before. Delia was her rock throughout the twenty-two hour labor.

The photo of Red, she'd kept close throughout her pregnancy set on her food tray. She lifted the picture with her left hand as she snuggled Lori Sky with her right.

"I have your redheaded baby, Red Anderson. Someday, if you love me enough, you'll come back to me. Then you'll have us both."

Acknowledgements

Thank you to the following individuals, who provided encouragement and recommendations during the writing process: Rae Neal, Myrna Kurle, L.K. Campbell, Gordon Kessler, Karen Cornell, Gretchen Craig, and Mark H. Jones.

Cover Design: tara@teaberrycreative.com

Specialized knowledge was obtained through interviews with Steven Roberts, Terry Crenshaw, and Michael Kurle. Richard H. Walton's book *Cold Case Homicides* was also a source of information for *Deadly Search*.

BOOKS BY Donna Welch Jones
*****
Sheriff Lexie Wolfe Novels
Killing The Secret-**Book 1**
Somebody is murdering the women who played on a championship basketball team twenty years ago. Sheriff Lexie searches for the link between the women that provoked someone to want them all dead.
Terror's Grip-**Book 3**
Lexie's right arm suspends above her, held by a chain attached to a two-inch clamp around her wrist. The chain trails through a broken cellar window. Her left hand fists and punches forward as if a boxing bag, or her captor's new face, dangles in front of her. Lexie's scream fills the cold darkness.
"I WON'T DIE WEAK"
Murder and Beyond-**Book 4**
Sheriff Lexie and Deputy Tye Wolfe are enmeshed in the strangest cases of their law enforcement careers. Two teenage girls vanish. Tye doesn't believe that Wendy is a witch. Lexie doesn't think the ocean swallowed Emma.

***Deranged Justice*-Book 5**

Local citizens panic when Sheriff Lexie doesn't solve a series of bizarre murder cases. She is removed from office pending an investigation of incompetence and criminal activity. An irrationally jealous woman and a man who demands custody of her adopted nephew add more turmoil to her life.

***Her Dying Message*-Book 6**

Sheriff Lexie's tears blur the body that lies face down on the rocks. Her scream catches in the wind and carries to the treetops. A family member was shot at close range—murdered. Her pursuit of evidence is hampered by a puzzling question. Why kill a good person for someone else's sins?

WOMEN'S SUSPENSE
Unbreak Their Hearts

ANTHOLOGIES
A River of Stories
Shades of Tulsa

Visit the author's website: www.donnawelchjones.com

Made in the USA
Lexington, KY
11 November 2019